ALSO BY MAURICE BROADDUS

The Usual Suspects

UNFADEABLE

MAURICE BROADDUS

KATHERINE TEGEN BOOKS
An Imprint of HarperCollins*Publishers*

Katherine Tegen Books is an imprint
of HarperCollins Publishers.

Unfadeable

www.harpercollinschildrens.com

Library of Congress Cataloging-in-Publication Data

Names: Broaddus, Maurice, author.
Title: Unfadeable / Maurice Broaddus.
Description: First edition. | New York : Katherine Tegen
  Books, [2022] | Audience: Ages 8-12 | Audience:
  Grades 4–6 | Summary: "A young graffiti artist learns
  to fight smart against the gentrification threatening
  her neighborhood"— Provided by publisher.
Identifiers: LCCN 2021024295 | ISBN
  9780062796349 (hardcover)
Subjects: CYAC: Graffiti—Fiction. | Street
  art—Fiction. | Neighborhoods—Fiction. |
  Gentrification—Fiction. | Community life—Fiction.
Classification: LCC PZ7.1.B75743 Un 2022 | DDC [Fic]—dc23
LC record available at https://lccn.loc.gov/2021024295

Typography by Carla Weise
22 23 24 25 26   SB   10 9 8 7 6 5 4 3 2 1

❖

First Edition

TO BELLA

AND WILDSTYLE. AND IMHOTEP.

YOU ALL INSPIRE ME.

I JUMP BEHIND A pillar as soon as I see the police car slow rolling down Clifton Street. I recognize the officer driving it by his trifling mustache, looking like he pasted squirrel fur on his upper lip. He's busted me a few times for tagging. Only once he rounds the corner and the car grumbles safely out of sight do I creep back around to the front. Middle school might be out, but it's not summer until my first tag of the year.

As I inspect my handiwork, I keep shaking my spray can. Not quite a nervous habit; I just like the way it rattles in my hand, like I'm a snake warning everyone that I'm out and about. The alternating red and green letters have black flames around them, spelling my name out along each pillar on the I-65 overpass, creating a 3D echo of the word. I don't just see colors, I feel them. Colors are all potential. They can be anything. It's all about how you mix them.

My name is Isabella Fades, a little bit of Black mixed with a little bit of white. My friends call me Bella, but out here in the streets, I'm known as . . .

"UNFADEABLE!"

Not my best work, but it'll do for now. Definitely not bad for a thirteen-year-old, if I do say so myself.

On the edge of the wall of the overpass is my main feature. A portrait of a Black woman in profile looking over her shoulder at the passing traffic. Her sepia skin color is darker than my tawny complexion—my light skin is the only trace left behind by my father. Her Afro flares out like the flames of the letters in *Unfadeable*. She has a way of owning everything about her. Her eyes are my masterpiece. Bronze with gold flecks in them. It took me forever to capture them the way I remember. Sometimes I let myself miss her.

I check the time on my prepaid cell. 1:45 p.m. Clouds crawl across the sky, thickening and darkening because Indiana's weather forgot that it's summertime not spring. I hope I can make it to the United

Northwest Area neighborhood association meeting before it starts raining. I've never been to one of these before. My rumbling stomach reminds me to pray that they will have have snacks at this thing.

I run my fingers through my hair and tie the bushy mess back with a scrunchie. My "Black Girl Magic is REAL" T-shirt over black leggings will have to do for this meeting because that's as professional as I'm going to get. Besides, I'm just about out of clean outfits.

Scrambling down the embankment, I wade though grass that sprouts nearly two feet high, like the yard of an abandoned house. The city hasn't sent out a prison work crew to mow it recently. I'm not surprised; it has a habit of forgetting our community. The way the highway carves up the blocks forces me to walk a long winding path from one part of the United Northwest Area—its full government name—to the other. Luckily, Clifton Street is the main corridor that runs through The Land, which is what the folks who actually live here call our neighborhood. Outside of my school, the Persons Crossings Public Academy, The Land is the only world that I know. It's magic. People call it The Land because the whole area used to be farmland. Now I almost twist my ankle walking along the uneven pavement of the cracked sidewalk.

Summer vacation's only as fun as you make it, you know? If I can't come up with my own adventures, I'd be stuck in a house complaining about how bored I am. That ain't me. I figure out what I have to do. I nod to a kid—maybe eight or nine, he stays on the block—fixing his bike, trying to make do with the parts he has. After fishing in the side pocket of my backpack, I hand him a small baggie of bearings.

"What's that?" He stares at the bag like I'm trying to hand him a cup of wasps. Oily splotches stain his white tank top. His shorts drape past his knees, matching his black socks against his Indianapolis Colts slides.

"Bearings for your bike."

"But Jared and 'em snatched them from me. Where'd you get them?"

"I found them." *Snatched from the bushes they guard like a bank vault where they tend to hide stuff* is probably more than he needs to know. "What do you care?"

"Oooh," he says, like I've just been called to the

principal's office. "Jared's gonna be mad."

He makes "mad" sound like it has three syllables.

"That's for me to worry about. I ain't scared." I glance over my shoulder, checking for anyone approaching by bike. Jared and 'em are only one thing wrong with the neighborhood. I can't quite put my finger on what's changed. "I heard some dudes were putting together a bike program over on Thirty-Fourth. Why don't you go up there and see if they can help you out?"

A still-uncertain look on his face—careful but not distrusting—he takes the baggie and upturns his bike to walk it up the block. He turns around for a second with his silent, "Thank you."

I don't even know how to respond to the boy properly. I never got to be a kid. My family has lived in one part or another of this neighborhood all my life. I remember being young, but that ended the day the police knocked on our door and I answered.

That's what led to me no longer having a home.

This is why I have only "associates." Friends are a risk I can't afford. They might find out about my situation. Even a "friendly ally," as my teachers like to call themselves, might feel the need to call the

5

Department of Child Services on me. I don't need anybody.

I swear I hear the sound of a bike skipping off the sidewalk around the corner and, fearing that Jared might be closer than I want, I run to the meeting. Still, going to this meeting is more a matter of survival . . . mostly because I was promised there'd be snacks.

I can't say I ever noticed the old Indianapolis Public Library No. 1 building much before the summer. With the number 1906 chiseled onto its cornerstone, it looked like another house overgrown with weeds and ivy. Ms. Campbell's on some committee to see about getting it on a historic registry because it's the oldest library building in Indianapolis. Since it's on our block, the city had forgotten about it, but she organized folks to help refurbish it into a community space. Me being here is her fault. She's always on me to do more stuff for the community. I'm not sure if that's me, though. *We're all in this together,* she always says like she's the neighborhood cheerleader. If anyone tries to call her by her government name, Essence Campbell, or anything else, they quickly get corrected. I'd call her my friend, but like I said,

I can't afford those. Friends share their lives, their secrets. But she's low-key, all right. I let her convince me to come to this meeting, but I'm really beginning to question her judgment.

For one thing, someone's got some poor planning skills. Two o'clock weekday meetings don't make sense. Naturally, the crowd outside the library is mostly a blue-hair convention, since the only people who can attend are retirees, the unemployed, and the people paid to be there. This must be how retirees and busybodies mix and mingle to meet people. Riverside community people, from the far side of The Land where my folks used to stay: a handful of business-people and property owners. It's like I'm walking the hallways of my school. I'm invisible. People acknowledge me enough to move out of my way, or not, but that's about it. They don't know me and barely make the effort to see me.

A few folks stroll along the sidewalk, with a couple older ladies dressed up like they've gotten lost on the way to a church meeting. The folks milling about on the sidewalk part as a woman, no taller than me, makes her entrance. Her hat, a wide-brimmed yellow thing trimmed with silk and rhinestones, bends and twists about her head. She wears it like a crown and half struts, yet doesn't quite meet people in the eye. Her eyes, always on scan mode, are like everyone's at my school when they bump into me: constantly searching for someone better to talk to. I hitch my bag higher on my shoulders and head up the stairs.

"Where do you think you're going?" Like a bouncer, this big dude by the door holds up a hand huge enough to crush coconuts. He has a barrel chest, and his face resembles a mug that's been broken and glued back together poorly.

"Into the meeting?"

"I don't think so." His voice is full of enough steel to build a cage, like when my teachers want to sound Serious. I think I'm supposed to be scared. "This here's grown-folks stuff."

"I know. Ms. Campbell invited me." I try to peek around him, but every time I move, he steps into my view.

"I don't think so." Even his voice sounds like he's looking down his nose at me. I mean, he is, since he's nearly two feet taller than me, but he doesn't hide that he's dismissing me.

I hate not being taken seriously. Hate. It.

But every now and then, my best play is to give them what they expect. I make my lip tremble. Just a level one tremble—subtle but noticeable. A level three lip tremble risks looking too over-the-top and he might not buy it. "My mom told me to meet her in there, but I don't see her. She told me to wait for her."

With a sigh, he first stares me up and down. Then he softens. Slightly. No one with feelings can take the lost little girl routine, no matter how tough they pretend to be. "Stay in back. Don't make noise."

"Okay. Thanks."

He acts like I am gonna shoplift a speech or something. I duck into the building.

The Indianapolis Public Library No. 1 still has most of its original shelves along the walls. The remaining books lining them are mostly from neighborhood authors. In each corner, chairs and love seats huddle around a coffee table. The space is open other than the former information, now receptionist's, desk. Rows of chairs face the wall on the other side of it.

I'm pretty sure everyone learns from middle school how to move through life. This meeting reminds me of a typical day in the life. People gather in small

packs, either with their friends or with the other pop-
ular kids. Each person tries to appear real important
to everyone else, like peacocks strutting around,
ready to stop and take a selfie at a moment's notice.
The grown folks here are no different. Already bored,
I shuffle off toward the back, near the aisle, always
ready to make a quiet and quick exit if I need to.

An older kid, maybe fifteen, sits next to an old
man. Probably his granddad who dragged him here.
I already can't stand him. Hot as it is outside, he's
got his letter jacket on. That thing is leather and it's
still summer in Indiana. But he needs the world to
see. He's big and lumpy, probably a football lineman.
Plus, he's got the nerve to manspread his janky legs
like he owns the place. Over there thinking he cute,
but he looks like a chubby spider monkey.

"What's up?" He gives a single cool flick of his
chin and scoots away from me like he's trying to give
me room. "Aaries Greyer."

"I didn't ask." Not wanting to study him any
closer, I scrounge around in my book bag until I come
up with my phone charger. Now that I'm inside, my
next mission is to find an outlet.

Smirking, Aaries nudges the old man. I thought

my complexion was light, but the old man's practically white compared to me. A mix of peach and tan, like sun-warmed sand. He's a sprawl of limbs tucked neatly into his chair. His collared shirt is unbuttoned, revealing a T-shirt touting a group called The Last Poets, who look like the great-granddads of a rap group. A red leather fedora dips low on his head.

The old man turns slightly. Even though the move is barely a glance, it's like he's taken me in completely. Settling by an outlet at the end of their row, I set my book bag between me and them like a wall and shift away so that I can pay attention to the meeting.

There aren't any snacks. Now I'm really irritated.

The old lady in the yellow hat breaks away from the group she was talking to. Her cane taps along the hardwood floor as she strides down the center aisle. Like a principal making an entrance, she hesitates, creating a show of nearing her seat, allowing people another moment to wrap up their conversations and head to theirs. She must always be expecting a meeting to break out at any second, since she takes a gavel from her purse. She smacks it once against the table. A sharp shot, like she fired a gun.

Something's about to go down.

"**GOOD AFTERNOON.** For those who don't know . . ." Her voice trails off a bit, giving her room to launch a petty smile. The kind of fake grin that means, if folks have gathered here, they should know who she is. "My name is Mattea Larrimore, board chair of the Northwest Planners neighborhood association."

Northwest Planners? I wonder if she's in the right meeting. We've been calling UNWA The Land since my mom was a kid. Now someone's renaming it Northwest Planners. The old man next to the spider monkey kid makes some disgusted noise, somewhere around a snort and half a fart. He's not pleased or impressed either.

"I speak on your behalf. The Voice of the People.

Thus, I hereby call this meeting to order. Let's begin with a reading of the minutes." Mattea obviously loves her rules and gavel pounding. The woman next to her drones on about past business, committee updates, and budget items as I realize someone is perched beside me.

Ms. Campbell has a way of sliding up like your favorite auntie. Vitiligo spreads along her hands. It's a skin condition some folks get where they start to lose their color. So, while most of her is a smooth ochre, her hands are speckled with splotches, and her fingers are pink like a white baby's butt. She's sort of the Big Momma of the neighborhood. One part candy lady, one part nosy neighbor.

"How are you doing, Miss Bella?"

"You said there'd be snacks." I don't mean to snap, but once my belly starts talking, my head is a mess.

"Mattea said we were over budget for snacks." Ms. Campbell tilts her head. When she looks at you, no matter how mad she may be, there's never any judgment. Opening her purse, she pulls out a bag of Takis and some Oreos. "Water fountain's over there."

"Thank you." There's no quiet way to open Takis, so I tear into the crinkling bag. Mattea's already eyeing Ms. Campbell's every movement like it takes her spotlight away.

"Think you can tell them about your mural idea?" Ms. Campbell half whispers.

"You sure I can't just keep tagging places? It gets the job done."

"Sure. But you wanted to know how to do a neighborhood art project. This is the way." Ms. Campbell also runs a sort of pantry/after-school snack program for the kids in The Land. Local farmers donate fruits and vegetable stuff that she cooks into small meals. Even when she's not trying to save the world all on her own, she has a way of making a person's idea bigger and somehow convince her to do the work, too.

"I guess."

"You got this." Ms. Campbell scoots over to a spot closer to the front. Mattea scowls at her the entire time.

I just wanted something to make me feel normal. That's how I ended up here at this boring middle-of-the-day association meeting. The thing is: I like to paint. It helps keep me sane. With school out, I don't really have that kind of outlet anymore. Well, if I'm not going to just tag places, I thought we could do some sort of art project. I didn't sign up for all of this, though.

Stifling a yawn, I lean back and grow more and more disappointed. The topics roll on: what street-lights are out, who did or didn't cut their grass, where abandoned cars and cracked sidewalks are causing problems. Complaining like it's work. By the time the chairs end the discussion over previous items, nearly forty-five minutes have gone by and the audi-ence has nearly dozed off. At least my phone is almost done charging.

"Is there any new business?" Mattea's voice sends icy needles up my back.

I stand up, brushing past the letterman jacket dude and his granddad to make my way to the mic up front. As soon as I move, it's like a spell is broken. Three men scramble to the microphone ahead of me, leaving me standing in the aisle. I catch Ms. Camp-bell out the corner of my eye. She waves at me. The first man asks about the state of the canal cleanup and is informed that the Reclaiming Our Waterways meeting is the following week.

The next man doesn't have a question. Armed with a stack of papers, he wants to spread the word

15

about the nonprofit he's starting to address violence in the neighborhood. The committee patiently waits out his commercial before cutting him off. Then the third man slides up to the microphone, buttoning his suit as he walks like he knows he's somebody. Mr. Important Pants tugs at his suit jacket as if smoothing out unseen creases, more to make a show and make sure all eyes are on him. I recognize that move from when I have to give a presentation at school.

"My name is Clarence Walls." He raises the microphone to keep from stooping down to it.

"People really need to make sure everyone knows their name," I whisper sarcastically.

"Says the person who spray-paints hers everywhere." Aaries doesn't spare me the slightest glance as he moves closer to the front.

He knows who I am.

"I . . . ," I start.

Aaries shushes me and leans forward to focus on Mr. Important Pants.

"I wanted to put a new piece of business before this fine board." Walls spreads his arms out like he wants to include the entire board in a hug. The wattage of his smile cranks up to one hundred. "As you know, my development company put in the Clifton Corner retail space."

"We thank you for your contributions to the community." Mattea joins many of the folks present in fanning herself. Even with only the couple dozen or so folks present, the room has grown hot enough to overwhelm the barely working air-conditioning.

"You're welcome." Clarence bobs his head as if accepting the applause only he can hear.

The way these two go back and forth with their extra politeness and praise, I wonder if they are going to start passing notes asking if they like each other.

"Anyway, the Corner is doing so well, we're running into a parking issue. I'd like to submit a proposal to this august body to possibly purchase the lot next to the center and partner with you to turn it into a parking lot."

"We look forward to reading your proposal." Mattea smiles and takes up her gavel, looking past me. "Any last items?"

"I have one." The microphone whines at the sound of my voice. Aaries comes over to adjust it to my height.

Covering the mic, he brushes his face near my ear.

"Watch out, she's easy to make an enemy of."

I eye him skeptically until he finds his seat again.

"What is it?" Mattea sounds like she's running out of patience. "We don't have time for any foolishness."

"It's summertime, and there are a lot of us out of school with not much to do in the neighborhood. I was wondering if there is a way to get an art project of some kind going. Like, for some classes or activities. To maybe do a community mural. I'm not sure how to go about getting money for it or anything, but I could—"

"That will be quite enough, young lady." Mattea smacks the table with her gavel. Once.

"But I—I wasn't done," I stammer. I feel the heat of all the eyes in the room turning toward to me. It gets hotter and muggier. My armpits itch, but I don't want to scratch with everyone already staring at me like I've done something wrong.

"Yes, you were. While we appreciate the passion of our young people"—her face is a wad of wrinkles over the microphone—"the fact of the matter is that any funding falling under 'art' or 'education' has already been allotted for infrastructure."

18

Ms. Campbell half rises out of her seat, but both me and Mattea wave her off.

"What does that even mean?" I crinkle my face in confusion. Like she went out of her way to string together words that mean nothing. But the folks on either side of her nod in stiff agreement, their faces equally Serious.

"This actually brings us to a last item of business I wanted to add to our agenda." Mattea directs me with her gavel. "Why don't you have a seat and learn a little something."

I refuse to return to my chair. I glare at each board member in turn. Like I said, I know when I'm not being taken seriously, and I hate it even more when I'm so casually ignored. It's grown-folks' way of trying to make me feel like I got no power. They don't respect the ideas of young people. We're background noise to them. If they want to test me today, I got time.

Mattea drones on. "I'd like to put before the board a proposal for additional funds to go toward the James Sidney Hinton Park."

"Is that even around here?" I blurt out. I actually get in trouble at school for talking out of turn. A lot.

At least once a week they send a note home about it for my mom to sign. Which means at least once a week I have to forge her signature.

"Of course it is. You'd know that if you were from here."

My face twists up so hard it hurts. I know this neighborhood. Ain't but one park over here and it's in the Golden Hill area. This "proposal" has a stank all over it. "How much money went to that so-called park in the first place?"

"We've already decided to allocate CISC's money from the TIF. The recipients have already been chosen." Mattea side-eyes me. "But to answer your question, we voted to dedicate a hundred thousand dollars toward the creation of the park."

"A hundred . . ." I ball my hands into fists. My fingernails dig into my skin so hard, they might draw blood, but I don't care. I just have all this anger that bubbles up from my belly like a sour mess and I need to throw it close on those in front of me. "How much more money could you possibly need if you spent so much already?"

Ms. Campbell drifts close behind me, resting her hand on my shoulder to calm me down.

All eyes bounce from Mattea to me back to Mattea. The older woman resists a sneer that tries to snatch my entire life. Luckily, she remembers the heat of the spotlight brought on by everyone's attention focusing on her. Inhaling a calming breath, she straightens taller in her seat with the dignified poise of a queen.

"The work has suffered numerous setbacks. You know how the Bible says that we 'wrestle not against flesh and blood, but against principalities, against powers, against the rulers of the darkness of this world'? Our darkness is the gangs." Mattea stops, allowing the murmurs to rise. She's been to church a time or two and is turning the room into her Amen corner.

As the supportive whispers begin to peak, she starts again. "Drug dealers came out to the park and burned up a lot of the playground equipment. I live right on the corner and ran out to try to stop them. I don't know what I thought I was going to do, but I had to do something. They called me a . . . Well, because there are younger ears present, I can't tell you what they actually said. It's what we've heard before, what we've seen before, and sadly, what we've grown used to. You know how some people are. They don't want to see anything good happen in the neighborhood. But I swear to you, I won't let them defeat us. *We* won't let them defeat us. *We* will show them. *We* will have our park!"

Most of the audience bursts out into applause. Mattea studies me. An evil smile curls her lips. I don't know if she was trying to intimidate me or rub my face in the moment, but now she done did it. My mom once told me that there was a group that came in and got two million dollars in grant money to do art in the neighborhood. They got all sorts of news attention and everything. I guess they brought in all these artists from all over the country to "beautify" our neighborhood. When they were done, all we got was a couple of murals. Not a single person in The Land even had a chance to show what they could do. Not even my mom. Nothing's changed. They're going out of their way just to make me feel ignorant. And I start to get mad.

I suck my teeth, grab my backpack and phone, then storm out the room.

She changed the topic like I'm not supposed to notice. And so I couldn't fuss without sounding like

I was defending drug dealers. She's up to something. I want to find this hundred-thousand-dollar park in my neighborhood. I'd like to claim that I have some heroic reason to get to the bottom of what it is. Yeah, I want to do my art project, but I'm also what my associates call a petty-ologist.

Mattea Larrimore's about to become my summer project.

I'M AN EXIT expert. If I'm mad enough to get ghost from a space, I need those left behind to know my mood. Usually that means a slammed door, even if at school that means an automatic detention. It's still worth it 'cause it gives me a sense of—what do they call it in relationships? Closure.

Not having a door to slam is one reason my dramatic storming out from Public Library No. 1 leaves me unsatisfied. The other is that I'm not sure where to go next.

The meeting leaves me so heated I can't think straight. But anger is my gift and Mattea is a raisin-faced Santa. I've already stormed over to the next block over before I realize where I am.

Golden Hill is one of the "old money" neighborhoods in Indianapolis. Whenever my mom talked about The Land, Golden Hill was never included. Fifty-four homes total, the oldest one dating back to the 1800s. Only the city's most prominent families live there. Golden Hill is so extra they have their own police guarding their little housing division. And their own park. Bertha Ross Park—with its rolling hills, old trees, and new playground equipment— lies firmly nestled in the Golden Hill neighborhood. That's on one side of Clifton Street—it might as well be a colony on Mars.

I live on the other side.

I head back to the blocks I know best. I grab my sketch pad from my backpack. Just having the Willow charcoal stick in my hand begins to calm me down. The girls at the bus stop giggle like we share a secret as I walk by. They never actually catch a bus. Whenever some dude strolls down the sidewalk, in go their earbuds. They're crazy protective of each other. I sketch them as knights of the neighborhood.

"Where you heading to, Miss Bella?" Ms. Campbell calls out from behind me. She must have followed me out of the meeting. I know she's barely forty, but she could pass for my older sister, except that her eyes give her away. They say she's seen and lived through a lot. She walks with a slight slouch whenever she's just going about her business, but as soon as she sees someone she knows, she straightens like an exclamation point. She fans herself with a magazine as we walk in the direction of her house.

Rather than keep shouting our business out in the streets, I cross over and stop along the sidewalk. "I don't know."

"You out here looking angry at the world." Ms. Campbell's cats meow while rubbing themselves along the brick edges of her porch. The largest one, Phineas, is a sleek black cat with too much belly and too short of legs who still manages to boss the other cats into submission. He climbs down the steps and curls himself between my legs until I bend over to scratch him behind his ears.

"I am." Though it's hard to be too mad with a cat purring in my hands.

"I got something for you." Ms. Campbell ducks inside and comes back out with a bowl full of Popsicles on ice. When I hesitate, she reaches into the bowl for a Popsicle.

I take a cherry one. Never blue raspberry. Blue fruit doesn't belong in nature.

"Let's try this again." Ms. Campbell stares at me with those bright brown eyes of hers full of everyone's secrets. "You doing all right?"

"Yeah." I study the ground. Her face so full of a mother-type love hurts too much to look at directly.

"You know, you can always crash here."

"I can take care of myself." I shrug my bag higher onto my shoulder.

"No one said otherwise. You'd be doing me a favor. Balance out the household with more female energy." Ms. Campbell reaches out, brushing my arm. "I have a new foster."

"I'll think about it." I draw away out of reflex. Ms. Campbell seems a little hurt and I feel my stomach twist up. "I will. Seriously."

"That's all I'm asking." Ms. Campbell smiles and it's like the sun chasing away the storm clouds overhead. The way my dad used to smile.

My dad was a manager at some foundation. I never quite understood what it was, but I knew it was important. Anytime someone mentioned its name, people stiffened or their eyes widened. It gave away money to "folks doing good work," he said. He was all suits all the time. Black suits. Blue suits. Charcoal suits. Mom was an art teacher, so she'd always add some color. She'd choose his ties or his pocket squares, always to draw out or complement the icy blue of his eyes.

I told myself that nothing was wrong. But by third grade, I'd come home and find mom sitting by herself in the living room alone in the dark. Curtains drawn. TV not on. There might be a couple pieces of half-eaten burnt toast on a plate next to her. She'd always had episodes like this. Dad would come home, send me to my room, and he'd take care of her. He had a way of drawing her out of her bad mood.

One time my mom disappeared for a week.

"Where'd you go?" I asked.

"Your mom . . . ," Dad started, but Mom shot him a look and he got quiet. He'd told me she went on vacation.

"Momma isn't always herself, baby," my mom told me. "You know how sometimes you get sick?"

All I could do was absently bob my head.

"Well, sometimes my brain gets sick."

"Like a cold?"

"Like a special kind of cold. It takes me to a dark place."

"But you got better?"

Mom made a noise like she didn't want to commit to an answer. Dad took her hand and she continued. "Sometimes I have to go to a special hospital to get better."

"A brain hospital."

"Exactly." She traced my nose with her finger. "One thing hasn't changed."

She made a thumbs-up sign in front of her and waited until I made the same gesture. Each of us pressed our thumbs to our chest and said, "My heart," at the same time. Then we pressed our thumbs together to make a little roof. "Is your house," we said in unison.

And I went back to my room.

Sometimes life is about the stories we tell ourselves—sometimes about ourselves—to get by. I used to tell my teachers that my mom got head colds every so often and had to go to a special hospital. They'd get this peculiar look on their face, like I *was an insect they'd seen before but were afraid to get near.*

I recognized the look. Dad had it right before he left us.

"Hey, do you know where the James Sidney Hinton Park is?"

"I hate that they still trying to call that mess a park." Ms. Campbell snorts, but it's a mean-sounding thing. I get the feeling she isn't exactly happy about how the meeting went down either. I begin to wonder if her coming after me also covered her storming out of there, too. If so, we have next-level exit expertise in common. "Yeah, it over there by the interstate. Off Twenty-Seventh Street."

"I never knew there was anything over there." Though I haven't been by there in a while, I scroll through my mental map of the neighborhood. All I can picture is a grassy field, but I recall talk about building houses over there. The city has been sprinkling money all over 30th Street and Doctor M.L.K. Jr Street in the last couple of years. I know that sounds good to most folks, but it feels like some unseen hand pushing people out who look like me.

"There's not. Ain't nobody ever over there." Ms. Campbell sounds all cryptic, like her words are supposed to mean something to me.

The way Mattea was running her mouth, about this park, something about that didn't make sense. I do the calculations of survival. The area where the park's supposed to be is only a fifteen-minute walk from here. I have time to make it there and back to my spot well before it gets dark.

"I'm heading over that way," I venture, hoping whatever she's holding back on might trip out.

"Just be careful. That area's all Paschall territory."

"Paschall?"

"Kevin Paschall, of the Paschall crime family. He owns most of the houses on that block. Some folks call him Pass."

Of course I've heard of Pass. I've never known his government name, though. Everyone always sees his black Corvette zipping about.

"Got boys over there like little soldiers. So just—"

"Be careful. I got it. I don't even know what I'm looking for."

Ms. Campbell looks me up and down, almost like she's seeing me for the first time.

"Bella, you're going to change the world. I can see that in you. But first you have to figure out who you are and how you want to move through this world."

～

What I love about The Land—there ain't no way I'm ever going to call it no Northwest Planners nonsense—is that there is so much life here. Continuing down Clifton Street, I pass the former Write On the Poetry Spot, a neighborhood open mic where poets used to gather every Friday night. Poetry's not really my thing—paints and colors I'm much more comfortable with—so I mostly went because they had free food that's pure fire made by cooks on the block. But it's closed now. My mother's last piece still decorated the outside, a faded mural that read, "Your Voice Welcome" with the letters filled with faces from the neighborhood. It's why I used to squat there until Pass bought it.

I wave at a couple in their backyard tending to their garden. I see them all the time, so we're familiar enough to smile at each other. The wife picks at a bush of roses. Arranged like a series of small fires, coral-colored peonies with occasional apricot- or peach-colored ones among them line their fence and sidewalks. The husband roots around in their garden, although all the vegetables look like weeds to me. At one point, I had counted over twenty gardens around The Land. Though it's not real organized, folks share food from their gardens. No one talks about how the neighbors band together to take care of each other.

A group of young boys and men work near what had once been an abandoned garage. They're scrubbing down the walls, stripping the old chipped paint from them so they could have smooth surfaces to work with. A scrap piece of spray-painted plywood serves as their temporary sign: "Coming Soon— Bikerz Shop."

Now I ain't gonna lie: The Land does have its problems. It's like there are a series of invisible boundaries I have to negotiate carefully. The more I wander away from Doctor M.L.K. Jr Street or Clifton Street or 30th Street or any of the main roads, the more I move into spaces fewer people care about. These invisible boundaries are one of the reasons I haven't been to this part of the hood in years. I duck behind a large tulip tree as I round a corner.

I don't see Pass's black Corvette parked anywhere.

But two boys on bikes buzz up and down the street, like someone has kicked a nest of thugs and they are out swarming. They might look like any other kids at play unless you know what to check for. Their eyes focus on the streets: strangers on the sidewalks, passing cars. They're lookouts, probably hoping one day to join up as members of Pass's crew. Which is bad for most of us 'cause that means they're rolling about trying to prove themselves. Worse, it being summer, they got time to kill. Coming out from behind the tree, I get a little closer and recognize them.

Fury and Jared Robinson. Nightmares by different daddies, who had their mother's last name. And it's my bad luck that they've spotted me.

4

"**WHAT ARE YOU** doing over here?" Fury carries a two-liter grape Faygo bottle full of water. His government name is Michael and his umber coloring makes his resting mean-mug face more intense and serious. No part of his tight fade connects with the scraggily thing on his face he wishes was a beard. He's a freshman in high school, but schoolwork's a struggle because—as he likes to shout to anyone who pays attention—that the streets "call out to him."

"Nothing. Just walking." I look straight ahead and keep my sentences short. I'm on a mission and not fishing for trouble. Most times life out here is about minding your own business and keeping your head down.

"You can't just walk these streets." Jared skids to a stop so close to me his tires kick up pebbles at my ankles. Unlike his brother, Jared is in my eighth-grade class, but he's older than me because he was held back a year. He has more of a taupe complexion, but that may be because he's always so ashy, it's like he's been dipped in dust. His uncombed, reddish-brown hair is a nappy mess. I don't know why anyone, much less Pass, would have him do anything for them. I wouldn't trust him with a bag of air.

"What, you setting up hood checkpoints?" I roll bored eyes toward him. Nonthreatening but not scared. It's the only way to maintain respect. Once they see you as scared, you ain't nothing but a target from then on out.

"Far as you concerned." Fury leans over his handlebars. Every movement he makes comes across like a show he's used to performing.

"Some stuff of mine came up missing. So I don't trust no one who don't belong around here." Jared studies me like he's trying to place a memory. I don't think he spotted me lifting his wheel bearings from his stash spot, but the streets have a lot of eyes. He got some nerve complaining about stuff coming up missing. He always in someone else's pocket. Rumor has it that he was also responsible for a series of break-ins around the neighborhood. He got it in his head that he wanted to start his own custom T-shirt company. Needing product, this fool broke into houses to steal shirts. Shirts.

"You know where James Sidney Hinton Park is?" Changing topics, my words sound more heated than I intended because I'm impatient. And I'm hot. Sweat rolls down my back, which further aggravates me.

"Don't know. Don't care." Fury drops words like a hammer. He ain't trying to have anyone argue with him.

"Them some fine tennies you got, though." Jared eyes my shoes like they the last piece of chicken at a BBQ.

"We ain't got time, J. We on the clock." Fury's mouth closes to a firm line.

"I can make time." Jared hesitates, glancing back at my shoes. He's always bolder when his brother's around to back him up.

"Boy, you steady stupid." So the thing about my mouth is that it has a habit of firing off before I can think about my choice of words. My tone catches him so off guard, Jared almost slips from his handlebars.

"What'd you say to me?"

A silence settles between us. It's like we're in a cowboy movie, waiting to see who will draw their pistol first. Basically, now's my chance to walk my words back a little, maybe even play them off as a joke. But thing is, I'm really irritated. And hot. And so not in the mood for his mess right now. "You. Steady. Stupid."

Jared's mouth screws up like he's determined to not swallow the sour thing in his mouth. He spits, off to the side. That's my cue to start running back the way I came, checking over my shoulder to see what kind of lead I have on them. Without hesitating, he pedals after me frantically. Fury sighs, all kinds of mad that his brother done stirred up some mess that he now has to cosign.

With my backpack heavy on my shoulder, I cut through a yard four houses down from their trap house. I'm mad at myself for letting my mouth side-track me from what I was supposed to be doing. Who knows when I'll be able to make it back this way, especially with these two clowns looking for me? They've been known to hold a grudge for a minute.

The overgrown bushes scrape my arms and legs as I run through them, but they cut off the path so that bikes can't pass. The boys loop back to the other end of the block and don't see me double back through the yard to head back to my side of the neighborhood.

The park will have to wait. I slow down to a trot, sure that I've lost them, and annoyed that I can't check out Mattea's story.

I want to figure out what she's up to, wipe that smug smirk off her face, and see what's up with the park situation. But already, it's starting to feel too big, like I tried jumping in the deep end of the pool before I had my first swimming lesson. Still, I won't let Fury and Jared stop me from anything I want to do.

I slow and struggle to get my breathing under control as I near where I've been squatting, the old William Ryder house. He was an artist from The Land. But since he died, the house has just been sitting there while folks try to figure out what to do with it.

Someone is waiting by the stoop.

5

As I roll up on him, the figure uncurls like a hooded gargoyle—despite the heat of the evening—and that raggedy boy, Aaries, from the UNWA neighborhood meeting, starts to walk toward me. I almost offer a weak smile but I catch myself. I know I'm cute, but that ain't the vibe we share. And I ain't trying to come off as scared neither.

"What you want?" I emphasize how annoyed I am to let him know that he is trespassing on my spot.

"Looking for you." His heavy-lidded expression doesn't even hint at being thrown off.

"What makes you think I stay around here?"

"You here, ain't you?" He shrugs. "Figured you'd pass by this way sooner or later."

"You stalking me?"

"You always so difficult?" His eyes flare open, like he's paying attention to me for the first time.

"Yes." I set my hands on my hips and wait.

Aaries just smirks. He fishes in his backpack and holds out a small envelope. "I'm supposed to give this to you."

"What is it?" I don't take it, only stare at it for a sec before turning my focus back to him. I want to see how long he gonna stay there holding it out.

"An invitation."

"To what?"

"I don't go reading other folks' mail."

"I don't go accepting invitations from strangers."

"Read it. Don't read it. I just had to deliver it." With that, Aaries sets the envelope on the ground and bounces.

He's long on his way before I bother to pick it up. After turning the envelope over and over in my hand, I open it. The note inside has an address and a time. Just over on 33rd Street. Tomorrow, at noon, with the words "Lunch provided" underlined.

I'll have to check my calendar to see if I'll be free.

Once Aaries is out of sight, I turn to go toward

the house. I pass a mound of brick, asphalt, and torn shingles piled and shaped into a statue of a face. Bowling balls act as its eyes, trails of stones as its hair. An uneven wooden fence, its white paint chipped and peeling, separates Mr. Ryder's former workspace from the rest of the yard. An awning of corrugated metal serves as the roof for those times he wanted to paint or sculpt outdoors.

I scurry around back and over the fence, out of eyesight of any nosy neighbors, to climb the mound of bricks Mr. Ryder had collected when the last grocery store in the area was torn down, to use in a project he never had a chance to complete. I pull back the piece of plywood covering the back patio door just far enough for me to enter.

Darkness blankets the whole house, except for the light outlining each of the boarded-up windows. The place is a museum of works in progress. Framed photos and paintings hang on the walls, obscured by the dim lighting. Mr. Ryder was sort of like a mentor for me. My mom introduced us, since he was her teacher, and he'd show me his art and drawings. Always excited to talk about color and perspective and lines, treating me like a real artist. Mr. Ryder wanted to bring the neighborhood together through art. He believed artists could change the world, no matter how young they are.

Some of his statues line the rooms like silent guards. I've named each one of them.

Grover stands closest to the door, with fingers of wound copper wire, a body of rivets, hair made from pipes, and a face molded from furnace scrap. Lounging in a chair by the window is *Sarah*. Elegant and poised, like she's ready to burst out into song at any minute. Rusted chain-link fence forms her body wound around tile flooring that gives the illusion of skin. Chains drape down as hair with a padlock for a barrette. Stationed by the stairs is *Wes*. A metal bucket forms his head, with twisted hangers dangling from it like metal dreadlocks. His body is shaped from furnace ducts. At night with all the shadows, they can be a little creepy. But most times when I study them I'm a little . . . awed. The work speaks to me, almost the same way that colors do.

Each stair creaks with my weight as I go upstairs, but I don't mind. They're like my early-warning system if I ever get unwanted visitors. Every sad squeak is especially loud in my ears without the background noise of air-conditioning. Or running appliances. Or any of the other noises of a living house. But with the floor layout memorized, I easily make my way to the back bedroom. My timing's perfect, and the streetlamp in the alley behind the house burns to life as evening finally gives way to night. I had been reading by candlelight, but after accidentally knocking over the candle one time and scorching my favorite shirt, I decided to risk removing the plywood from just the bedroom window.

Sitting my book bag in the corner, I fish out the leftovers I'd scavenged throughout the day. I make space next to a sculpture I made in my Persons Crossings Public Academy art class—a figure of a girl reading a book. It took me forever to get the hair right. I always keep it next to my bedroll. As I eat, I grab my sketch pad and draw the image of Fury and Jared chasing after me on their bikes. I make their teeth extra pointy, hungry steel traps in their mouths. When I reach for some ink to trace the linework, the invitation tumbles out. I turn it over in my hands a few times. I'd have to be careful. And smart. There were all sorts of predators out in the streets. It wouldn't hurt to not go at them by myself.

Maybe I could use some allies.

AT FIVE TILL noon the next day, I'm standing on the sidewalk outside the address the invitation directed me to. Like many of the houses around here, it reminds me of the one I grew up in the Riverside part of The Land. This one is a white two-story home whose paint has started to flake away in large chunks. A porch wraps around the front, its columns and the brick base all freshly painted a strange shade of rust. The dark gray porch floor also has been recently touched up. I must've passed the house all the time during my walks around the neighborhood. I guess I never take much notice if people don't come and go on the regular.

"Girl, what are you doing out here?" Ms. Campbell

asks from the other side of the street.

"I got an invite for this address." I wave toward the house, though suddenly my feet have second thoughts about going toward it. "Lunch at noon."

"Whoa, M invited you over? You must rate. The wizard doesn't invite just anyone behind the curtain."

"Who's M?"

"I don't know how to describe him. If you're doing something on the block, then he's all up in your business."

I grow more curious. Maybe he has the lowdown on Mattea. "Well, at least you know where I was going in case I turn up missing."

Ms. Campbell laughs. "You'll be all right. Aaries works for him. I barely see him around here most days."

"Around here?"

"I told you I had a new foster." She turns to go back into the house. "Don't be late for your lunch."

On this M's porch, a collection of doors lean next to one another. Each door has been used as a canvas, with some picture painted on it dedicated to the story of the neighborhood. One's obviously by William Ryder, with carved-up and crushed cans creating the portrait of a girl at play. Other doors feature the gardeners. The one that's everything displays Indianapolis police officers dumping Black bodies into graves at Crown Hill Cemetery. I remember when all the police shootings around the country had the community shook. The last door is a piece by my mom. A picture of kids playing curb ball under the words *Better Days*. The girl in it is achingly familiar.

When I knock on the screen door, a letter tumbles out of the overstuffed mailbox. Whoever lives here hasn't collected it for days. Maybe even weeks.

A mad scrabble of nails along hardwood floors followed by harsh dog yelps cause me to take a step backward. I shift my backpack to my other shoulder, preparing to book it if need be. Some muffled shouts try to drown out more barking before Aaries opens the door.

"Thmei, let her in." Aaries's hair has been drawn up, two braids tied together on top of his head. A pit bull strains against his grip on her collar.

"Who hurt you, Aaries?" I can't help but stare at

the handiwork on top his head. "Someone got your head looking like you live in Whoville."

"You got jokes, I see." The dog tugs against Aaries, but his arm barely moves. "You good with dogs?"

"Yeah." Dropping to a knee, I inspect the dog a little closer. "She bite?"

"Biting's the least of your problems." Grinning, Aaries releases the leash.

Thmei charges. Full tilt. I barely get my arms up before the weight of her slams into me. Her tongue lashes desperately. Managing to crawl up on my knees, I get in maybe two solid pets before Thmei, all coiled muscle, bowls me over again to better lick me.

"That's enough, Thmei." Aaries attaches the leash and tugs her away. He can hardly say anything else over his laughter. Thmei hops as she walks, like she hopes to swipe a lick at him if he misses a step.

"She's not the best security dog." I wipe myself off, then rub my hands on my jeans.

"She barks a good game, though. If a thief hears a pit bull bark, they rethink they life choices. But if they get in, it's over. She just rolls over for belly rubs. Come on, he's back here."

Aaries's heavy footfalls make the floorboards

groan. The front room and dining room bleed together, forming one large open space. The hardwood floors appear recently polished, with only fresh scratches from Thmei running across them. African tapestries full of elephants and giraffes dangle along the walls. Tribal masks and other, more modern artwork hang alongside them. The modern art clashes with the mood of the room, but I recognize most of the works from local artists.

Every other surface—from the dining room table to the coffee table—is littered with empty pizza boxes.

"Excuse the mess," Aaries says.

"Just so I got this straight, you invited me over, were expecting company, and you didn't even *attempt* to clean up?" A strip of carpet runs along the hallway, red and ratty, having lost the battle to Thmei. The drywall has cracks, thin fissures cutting through the plaster patches. The trim warps, bulging outward with protruding nails barely holding it in place.

"You right, you right. But he didn't want to put on airs." Aaries points to a door. "He in there."

I eye the hallway warily. My hand reaches for the can of Mace I keep tucked in an easily reached pocket along my backpack. Just in case. Strains of jazz music flutter out from behind the door as I nudge it the rest of the way open.

"Right on time." The old man doesn't bother turning around, instead facing a series of computer monitors. One of the screens has a montage of camera feeds from around the house, inside and out. His red leather fedora hangs from a coat stand next to a workstation of three large monitors.

"For free lunch, I'm always punctual," I say.

"I'll make a note of that." The man turns around. Long spidery fingers keep dancing along his keyboard with the skill of a concert pianist. His hair puffs out, graying about the temples, a combed-back Afro. A wispy beard dangles from his chin, and a gray film shimmers along his eyes like they've captured moonlight. He gestures to three boxes spread out on the coffee table in front of a couch. "Help yourself."

"Let me guess: pizza." Another large square of carpet—tan with smears of gray as if someone poured out a bowl of cigarette ashes and rolled around in them—is spread under the wood coffee table. Winterizing plastic sheets still cover the windows, held down with duct tape. I plop my backpack in front of the couch. My can of Mace remains within easy reach.

"I got both kinds: pepperoni and plain cheese." Granddad waves his arms out. "But first, introductions. Unless you make a habit of eating with strangers."

"Just because I know a name doesn't mean you're not a stranger. I assume everyone's fake."

"Well, you should never be afraid to let people know who you are. You should never be afraid to sign your work."

"But I already . . ."

He grins like he was waiting for me to get his joke.

I thumb toward Aaries. "He seems to think he knows who I am."

"I like her." He nods at Aaries, who's posted up in the corner. "You have to forgive him. He investigates whatever strikes him as curious."

"Your grandson?" I ask between loud, sloppy bites of pizza.

Aaries snickers but keeps his face in his laptop.

"Not quite. More of an intern. My name is Menelik Paschall. Menelik is Ethiopian for 'son of a wise man.' My friends call me M."

"And my middle name is MindYaOwn, ancient

Egyptian for 'lack of judgment.'" Since he's obviously used to impressing people with how much he knows, I try to keep from rolling my eyes. My arms stop from crossing on my chest as the rest of his name hits me. "Wait a second. Did you say Paschall? You related to Pass?"

"He's my brother."

I freeze, calculating my next move and possible escape routes. The Paschalls are bad news. Not a single member of their family has ever been convicted of a serious crime even though they've been linked to bodies dropping and everyone knew their trap houses moved serious weight.

Reaching for my bag, I prepare to bounce. I scoop up two slices of pizza for my trouble. "I'm out."

"BEFORE YOU CUT out." M raises a lone bony finger. "Let me make you a proposition: finish our chat and keep all the pizza. Consider it a consultation fee."

My hand hovers over my bag's handle. "Consultation for what?"

"You're bright and have opinions. I just want to see what you think about a few things." M is facing me, but I can tell he's not quite tracking me. More like he's either following the sound of my voice or can see a little but not real well.

"Only if you tell me what I want to know." I relax a little and settle back into the chair. If nothing else, Ms. Campbell would never let one of her fosters hang around with someone she knows is dangerous.

"That's exactly what I mean. Smart." Though they never seem to focus on anything in particular, his eyes follow the movement of my backpack. "First of all, I like to know who *I'm* dealing with. I heard you have tags all over town. How long you been painting?"

"Two years." I wipe a strand of dangling cheese from my chin. I feel like I'm in a game of chess with him. Each of us making moves, testing each other's strategies, before we reveal our true plan.

"Go to school?"

"Persons Crossings Public Academy."

"Middle school, eh?" M cocks his head like he's appraising jewelry. "Seventh grade?"

"Going into eighth." I smile.

"I was close. Got any hobbies?"

"You looking to stalk me?" My tone's more playful than I feel. I ain't trying to be interrogated like I'm in police custody or nothing. And he's still a Paschall. But his vibe feels genuine, like he's actually interested in me. Making myself more at home, I unpack my charger from a side pocket and search the wall behind and beside the couch until I find an outlet to plug in my phone. If I'm gonna be here for a minute, I might as well charge up.

"Just taking an interest." M seems to catalog my actions, making a mental list of observations without commentary. For some reason I can't put my finger on, I like that. The way he pays attention to everything while letting me be, with no judgment. Then the rising wail of a trumpet breaks my attention.

"What's this you listening to? It sounds like someone is choking a frog."

"It's *Sketches of Spain*. By Miles Davis. My favorite musician. The man was a genius."

The notes hit me like thunder exploding in my ear, mostly because of the lightning flash of memories it triggers. My dad dragging us out to "Jazz in the Park" during the summer. Other than a few old heads, me and my mom were the only two brown faces out there.

"The man needs to hit a proper note once in a while. Maybe pick one and stick to it instead of playing all of them at the same time."

"I'm not having this conversation with you. You ain't ready." An expression of exaggerated pain crosses M's face, like he's supposed to be all in his feelings. He lowers the volume on the music. When I glance Aaries's way, he pretends he's focused on the laptop he's working on. But I get the feeling he's M's extra set of eyes.

I reach for another slice. "What can you tell me about Mattea?"

"Straight down to business. I like that." M pushes back into his seat like he's trying to find a comfortable spot. "What was your impression of her?"

"Why you want my opinion?" Even though I'm trying not to sound skeptical, I can feel that my eyebrows arch so hard my face aches.

"Fresh eyes. As you might have guessed, mine aren't so good anymore," M says.

"What about Aaries?" I tilt my head toward his corner.

"I already know what he thinks of things."

"Well, I don't like Mattea Larrimore. At. All. And she don't think much of me."

"That so?" M can't hide the flash of amusement on his face. "I can live with good work for the wrong reasons. What else?"

"I don't know who she thinks she is. She talks down to people. Treats everything like a press conference or something."

"You think she's lying?"

"She's too quick to spin stories. That whole thing about facing down drug dealers was so extra."

"An unsolicited lie." M turns his milky eyes toward me.

"Something like that. She sprinkled in too many details."

"That what made you suspicious of her explanation? I thought that was the mark of a true story. Make it sound more real."

From the way M says that, I can tell he's testing me. But I'm on to how he plays now. "Only amateurs start adding in extra details. Especially stuff no one asked for. Nah, that story was about her. She wanted some street cred or something."

He smiles. If I was being tested, I've passed. "But what would she have to gain?"

"Make herself look good to folks, for one. The rest was for effect. Pure drama. Distract folks, make them forget my question. And that was something else that bothered me: Mattea never mentioned how much the new proposal was for. You notice how no one asked?"

"You don't miss a trick." M's mouth breaks into

a wide grin. His teeth vary from slightly yellow to dark, like a mouth full of garden stones.

"You get caught slipping out here—" My words get cut short by Thmei nudging the door open, spilling into the room, and jumping into my lap. The dog's too big for my legs, but Thmei keeps scrabbling for footing anyway. Her body sprawls all over me when she finally relaxes.

"Thmei, get down. I'm going to put you up if you can't act right." No stranger to barking a good game, M raises his voice but doesn't move in her direction.

"Where'd you get her from?" Through her constant squirming, I pet her as best I can.

"She ain't mine. A neighbor moved and her new place don't allow pets. I said I'd take her until she could get resituated. She ain't staying long."

"How long's it been?" I dodge Thmei's excited tongue.

"Four months."

I scratch behind Thmei's ear. "They ain't coming back."

When I hear them out loud, the words hit harder than I expected. That moment when I first heard about Daddy.

"Is your mom here?" one of the police officers asked. They were so tall. Their uniforms navy blue and crisp, not a crease on them. Their faces were a weird combination of expressions. Hard and serious, like concrete. But around the edges, when they saw me, they softened with sadness. Mom came rushing to the door.

"Is there a problem, officer?" Mom stepped in between us.

"Chantal Fades?"

"Yes."

I held on to the back of her leg. There was something safe about hiding behind the folds of Mom's dress. I wanted to run and hide in my room. I didn't want to leave her alone. I needed to know why they were here.

"Can we talk, ma'am?" The closer officer glanced at me and then back to her.

"Whatever you have to say to me, you can say to the both of us. We face things." Mom always said that life was hard and there was no sense in running from it or shielding me from it. Her and Dad often argued about her ways of doing things.

The officers turned to each other. I knew that

look. Whenever me and whoever my teacher had assigned as my partner had to decide who went first to give their presentation. A quiet argument of their eyes. The closer officer lost.

"May we come in?"

"We can do this, whatever this is, right here." Mom was not a fan of police. We'd already had that talk. There was no way she was going to let them in the house to "have a free look around to find something to use against us."

The officers flashed a look between them like they had to go with their plan B. "Ma'am, do you know an Eric Turner?"

"He was my husband." Mom's legs trembled, like the way the officer said his name almost knocked her over. "What happened to him?"

"Ma'am, his family asked us to notify you." The officer looked down at me again. "There was a car accident. He didn't make it. I'm so sorry."

The other officer stepped closer as if ready to catch Mom.

But her legs locked into place, a tree searching for its roots to keep from tumbling over. She brushed *off his arms before they reached her.*

*"Where's Daddy?" The word came out of me in
a soft squeak.*

"Your daddy's left us, baby," Mom whispered.

"When will he be back?"

"He ain't coming back."

And just like that, my childhood ended.

"She *better* come get this dog." M swipes at the air, trying to shoo away the dog. It snaps me out of the dark memories my thoughts had fallen into. Thmei ignores him. "I already had to rename her. Thmei's the name of the Egyptian goddess of truth. I ain't calling no dog 'Hera.'"

"No wonder she don't listen. She don't even know her own name," I say. M pauses for a second, his head tilting as if I'd said something profound. I read somewhere that when dogs do that, it is because they are trying to process new information. Maybe people do it, too.

I squeeze Thmei's face between my hands. "Your momma ain't coming back. No she isn't. But who's a good dog?"

Breaking free of my grasp, Thmei flicks her tongue at my face.

"Thmei, get down. She must want food." M spins around toward Aaries, who's already returning with a new bowl for the dog.

"Let me ask you a question. Besides your tired old-people music, what's this little meeting all about?" I point toward his elaborate workstation. "I don't know how any of this city stuff works." I throw my hands up. "CISC. TIF. Y'all speak another language. No wonder things are so messed up."

"Don't pretend you aren't smart. You don't wear dumb well," M said. "Ask your questions."

"All right, what's a TIF?"

"TIF stands for Tax Increment Financing. Think of it like the neighborhood bank account. Imagine some community leaders got together and told the politicians downtown that their community needs to control its own destiny and be in charge of fixing itself. And the politicians responded by setting aside so much of the tax money in an account for them to decide how to use it."

"That sounds . . . great?" I raise my voice at the end to turn the statement into a question. I'm not sure if I'm understanding everything.

"In theory. But let's say ten years pass and no one lets anyone in The Land know it's there. Hundreds of thousands of dollars stack up, yet the people who do know about it only *claim* to live in your neighborhood."

"Wait, you're telling me that we have access to that much money and The Land still looks like it does? All them boarded-up houses? Everything so run-down? And folks around here know about this?"

"I doubt most people know what's going on with the TIF. Or who has control . . ." M lets his voice trail off.

"It's Mattea, isn't it?" This woman is working every last one of my nerves. She better not be sitting on *tens* of dollars, much less a mil, and want to start talking about not having any money for a tiny art program. She's about to make my list a second time.

"The way the TIF was set up, CISC—the Central Indiana Support Corporation, one of the ways money gets pushed through the city—funnels money to it but nothing can come out of it unless a vote passes the governance committee. And the governance committee meetings aren't ever announced, so no one can propose new ideas."

"Ms. Campbell?" My voice cracks with disappointment.

"She's the only real voice of community in that space. The way I read things, she keeps getting shut out or outvoted. The program used to be more flexible, but lately, it seems a lot of the money has been going to Clarence Walls."

"Walls? I don't understand."

"My mind works in all sorts of crooked ways." M leans his chair against the wall, bobbing his head to music only he can hear. With his eyes still shut, he whispers, "If I were to ask you how you would shuffle money around in the community under everyone's nose, how would you do it?"

I tap my chin for a moment. I remember what my mom told me about those artists who came in to do murals and I snap my fingers. "Hire someone. From outside." Then my whole face collapses in realization. "This whole game is rigged."

"No need to get all worked up. I'm just explaining the nature of the game."

"I'm not worked up." I pace back and forth. My head hurts. I keep thinking about my mom. How she kept believing the system was too big. That nothing could change. That she was weak. But I'm not power-less, and I'll never let them make me helpless. "What can I do about it?"

"Why did you go to the meeting in the first place?" M asks.

"You always answer questions with questions?"

"It's part of my teaching method."

"What's the class? How to dodge answering things? Besides, you heard what I said. I was trying to get money to start an arts program. It's my neigh-borhood, too."

"Why you?"

"Why not me?"

"There you go." M smiles like I've said the magic words he wanted to hear. "Speak more on that."

"I wanted to do something for The Land. I grew up here, over on the Riverside half." Riverside's the neighborhood that makes up the south side of UNWA community, named after the old Riverside Amusement Park. My mom told me they let Black folks in only one day a year back when her mother was young. Her voice always sounded hurt whenever she talked about it.

"You like the neighborhood griot," M says like a doctor making a diagnosis.

"Gree-oh?" I pronounce the word, turning it over in my mind the way I do whenever I find a word I don't know. Adding it to my arsenal. "What's that?"

M types the word, the font on the screen enlarged enough for me to read from across the room. "Like a historian. You know all the stories of the community."

"Like I said, my mom raised me here. She was always telling these old stories."

M shifts his head slightly, his expression unreadable. Whatever dances in his head, he changes topics. "I used to be a private investigator. Put all my lawyer education to practical use. Till my eyes started going bad."

"So, you up in here like some sort of retired Batman?" My curiosity's going again. There are pieces not connecting right. Pass's brother a lawyer turned PI. Ms. Campbell says he's cool, but these can't be smooth Thanksgiving family dinners. I empty the first box of pizza of its last piece.

"Now I mentor a few young folks."

"I guess that makes him prepubescent Robin."

"Hey!" Aaries glances up. "I'm sixteen. And a half."

"And a half, huh? Anyway, someone like you

didn't just invite me over for conversation and a slice. What else you want?"

"I'd like to hire you for a job."

"What . . . sort of job?" My guards go up. I'm suspicious of any job for a Paschall. And just as afraid to turn them down outright.

"You want to learn more about Mattea and what's going on? I want to pay you to figure it out."

"How?"

"You know the first thing I do when I show up in a new space? I get out and walk those streets. See and feel it for myself. How the people live, react, and move about. I learn the background rhythms of a place and people, I can tell when someone's trying to sell me some bull. You walk these streets all the time, but I bet you rarely take the time to know folks."

I take a moment to let his words sink in. "What's the second thing you do?"

"Me? I like to investigate things going on around here. If one project smells fishy, others might, too. May lead to an entire bad batch that needs to be recalled for the safety of community. I just want you to canvass the neighborhood. Learn who your neighbors are. What businesses are here. Who's doing what."

"I understand. I just don't know where to start."

"I always say start where you are and use what you have to do what you can. And right now, you don't know what all you have." M grabs a clipboard with a sheet of paper on it. "Here's a list of people and places to visit."

I roll my hand, hinting for the magic words I want to hear.

"I pay ten bucks an hour. Plus"—he gestures at the pizza boxes—"your consulting fee."

"Okay." I start packing up the second box and tuck it under my arm. The remaining slices slide to the bottom. "But I can't hang with pizza all the time like you two."

"It's the meal of champions." M half throws his hands up like he knows he's already lost this battle. "What do you like to eat?"

"Burger King." I snap my fingers as I remember something also. "And Oreos."

"A dinner fit for a queen." M turns back to his monitors. "See you tomorrow. Be careful, though. You start kicking over rocks, what you might find under them may decide to kick back."

8

LEAVING M'S PLACE, I head toward Clifton Street. The first place on the list of addresses he put on a clipboard for me is Clifton Corner down on 30th Street, a place I'm quite familiar with, since I begin most of my mornings there. I wave at the neighborhood mechanic. The old man's always half buried in the engine of an old truck he never seems able to keep running. Anyone else's car, though? For about twenty bucks, he can make it do anything.

A sharp bark startles me.

When I turn around, Thmei strains at her collar, her stubby legs scampering like propellers, her overgrown nails clacking against the sidewalk. Aaries clutches the leash, not stressed in the least.

"What are you doing?"

"Taking Thmei for a walk." Aaries has a worse poker face than I have. He can't even pull off playing dumb.

"You happen to go for a walk this way? Right now?"

"Thmei's got to go when she's ready. Or else she drops boo-boo all over the house and I ain't trying to clean that up."

The dog doesn't look like she has to do her business. Thmei stretches up on her hind legs, anxious for me to pick her up. I drop to a knee to squish her face. "I can't play right now. I have work to do. Alone. Why don't you walk my babysitter somewhere else?"

"I'm not your babysitter," Aaries objects.

"Bodyguard?"

"Not . . . exactly. M mentioned you should be careful out here. I . . . thought you ought to have backup."

"Uh-uhn. That's not going to work for me. I've been out here taking care of myself just fine." I stand and start walking. Quick enough that Aaries has to scamper a bit to catch up.

"I'm just saying you don't have to."

"I don't need you over here cramping up my style." I wave him off.

"Think of me as a—"

Before he decides to declare himself my bodyguard or something, I whirl and stare at him dead in the eyes. My raised finger cuts him off. "Sidekick. You strictly sidekick material."

"I'm older," Aaries says.

"Bigger, too. And?" I glance up and down him like he's small, chest puffed out like he's supposed to be somebody. "You follow my lead or you can go home."

"You always this difficult?"

"What's my name?"

"Bella Fades."

"What's. My. Name?"

"Unfadeable?"

"There you go. Come on."

I ain't going to lie. I do feel better knowing Aaries is behind me. But this is my show. As long as he understands that, we'll be cool.

Thmei stops short of Clifton Corner. The way

she sniffs, maybe she's finally ready to do her thing. Her timing's perfect, as if she were the kind of dog who *really* took forever to find the exact bush to drop off on.

"You stay here. I'll duck in for a quick second. Be right out."

Letting the doors hiss shut, I don't give him a chance to protest. I wander about the lobby, really noticing it for the first time. Clifton Corner is a bunch of stores mixed with apartments that no one had asked for. It's like renting a room over a mall. It has that weird design that all the new buildings around town seem to have, with bright pastel panels mixed with brick. Since it's part residential, the lobby is open twenty-four hours. I've been here before—to go in, brush my teeth, and wash up before most folks even hit their Snooze button—but now I'm really noticing it.

"What are you doing?" Clarence Walls startles me as he slinks out of his office. The usual growl to all teenagers, followed by that look like I'm not supposed to be here without an adult in tow. He's wearing a custom brown pin-striped suit with a deep auburn shirt matching his stripes, tie, and pocket square.

The man next to him sports an equally expensive suit and carries a large enough Bible to announce what he does for a living from across the hall. He looks vaguely familiar.

"Looks like you're about to have your hands full, so I'll leave you to it." Glancing at me without really seeing me, the minister excuses himself. Obviously, I'm not serious enough business for him to really pay attention to.

Every muscle in my body tightens as Jared and Fury step out from behind the pastor.

We lock stares, our eyes darting back and forth to see how we'll play this, who'll make the first move. Jared starts to step forward, but Fury flicks his hand out, barely brushing his brother's leg. It stops him dead in his tracks.

"Thank you, pastor. My boys will give you a tour of the place."

"It was nice meeting with you, brother. It's good to see God's work in the youth today. Your mentoring program is an inspiration to the community."

Only then do I catch how Fury and Jared are dressed. Not like they're going to church or anything, but like they're on their way to a job interview.

Khaki pants, black polo shirts, almost like a school uniform. The way Jared fusses at the collar, he can't wait to be out of it.

"Right this way, Pastor." Fury leads the way.

The pastor follows, but Jared lingers for a heartbeat. He bumps my shoulder as he steps past. He must want to catch these hands, but Walls cuts me off before I can slam my clipboard into the back of the boy's head. Instead, I say "Is your bike a little off? I bet a brother could use some new wheel bearings. I wonder where I could get some of those."

Jared whips around on his heel. He may have stolen that kid's wheel bearings, but at that point they were his. And I stole from him. That kind of thing couldn't go unanswered. His hands ball into fists. Fury catches him by the arm.

"Not now. We're on the clock," Fury says.

Jared's stare slow burns into me, but he turns back to the pastor.

"What can I do for you?" Clarence Walls lets his fake smile fade as the good reverend leaves. He returns his full attention to me, ready to do a stop and frisk.

"Just checking the place out." I hold up my

clipboard. "I'm taking a survey of the neighborhood. I'm supposed to tally the good work going on."

That throws him off. He angles his head toward me with a quizzical expression, like he's trying to calculate how much charm to turn on. He turns on an uncommitted smile in case I might be kin to someone important. "You look familiar."

"I was at the neighborhood meeting."

"Yes, yes, that was it. The art girl." He lowers the wattage of his smile.

"Yeah." I try to study as much of the lobby as possible while keeping Walls in my peripheral. People trickle in through the doors. Only a handful, barely enough to justify opening most of the stores. "You mentor?"

"The boys come in for an hour or so each day. We talk and I give them their assignments for the day. They're good soldiers."

"I bet they are." I'm not sure what M wants me to see. The floors, even after so many months, still gleam like new. Many of the storefronts remain empty, still trying to make up their mind what they want to be. "This must have cost a lot to build."

"Nearly twelve million dollars. But I've had a lot

of partners. That man who just left was Reverend Charles Taft, one of the—"

"Oh, that's who that was." I snap my fingers. But since I'm inside, I don't spit. Taft is the pastor of Nu Land Missionary Baptist Church. He looked so familiar because he seems to always find himself in front of television cameras where he blames the folks in our neighborhood for our problems. One reason why I've struggled to believe in anything much these days. "Yeah, I've heard of him."

Walls slips into self-promotion mode out of reflex. "Well, we just reached an agreement where his church will have access to some of our spaces for meetings."

"This all sounds good." I jot down the information while continuing to study the center. At midafternoon, I expect a little more going on from at least the folks who live here.

"How good of friends are you with Mattea?" I ask.

"*Ms. Larrimore*"—he emphasizes her name to correct me—"and I are good friends. Longtime colleagues and partners."

"So, you were a part of the Hinton Park project?"

"Only a little. We give to a lot of neighborhood projects."

I make a show of writing on my clipboard. "I'm still trying to figure out why there's no money for a simple arts project."

Walls makes a weird gurgling noise. "Well, I certainly have no control over how money gets spent."

"These apartments look nice." I try to shake him off his game by changing the subject abruptly.

His grin amps up a notch, like a proud dad about to brag on his child making honor roll. "Those are my pride and joy. I believe that everything we do, no matter what we build, we have to give back to the community. Those spaces are strictly reserved for low-income housing."

The words sound well-rehearsed to me. His sales pitch. "How much they run per month?"

"Fifteen hundred." His smile shows off all of his teeth. Pearly white, ready to snap shut on the nearest prey.

"Fif—?" I barely stop myself before a barrage of cusswords tumble out. "What kind of poor folks you hang out with?"

"I don't know if you understand what all is in motion to make this kind of operation work. We have a tax credit program to . . ."

Blah. Blah. Blah.

My eyes glaze over. Some people throw around a lot of words, hoping people will quit caring and believe whatever. I butt in to stop his speech. "I don't know if I understand how that works. So if I make a lot of money, I can get a spot. That about it?"

"See? It's too complicated for you." His smirk fades. Grown-ups make this mistake all the time. They think we don't care about stuff going on. But it's our world, too. Miss us with the nonsense.

"I don't think it is." I press the clipboard to my chest in my crossed arms. "It sounds like people are making up the rules as they go along. I've played enough recess games to know that never works out for anyone except the person in charge."

My mind starts to work in all sorts of crooked ways. Like how bribes and favors might be being passed out like candy at Halloween, but only certain folks know to even dress in costume. Clarence Walls just got added to my list.

"I think it's time for you to go." Walls steps closer

to me, trying to intimidate me with his height. I lock eyes with him to let him know I ain't scared. I don't care how old or tall he is.

Thmei barks from the entrance. From the side of my eye, I see Aaries allowing her leash to stretch tight.

"We good in here?" Aaries asks.

"Yeah." I wait for Walls to blink first. "We all good."

9

"I CAN TAKE care of myself. By myself," I say once I get outside.

"You sound like I did before I settled in with Ms. Campbell."

"It's just that . . ." My voice trails as I try to figure out the right words. "People learn my story and they just want to protect me. They treat me like I'm fragile."

"I'm none of that. I'm just . . . what did M call me? Extra support if you want."

"I don't want."

"In that case, I'm just out here walking Thmei." Aaries shrugs.

I never considered myself much of a dog person.

Or a cat person. Or a pet person, period. Animals are like babies: cute and all, but I need to give them back to someone after I'm done playing with them. The idea of something depending on me, that was a little too much. Still, Thmei has a scruffiness that I like. I don't have to give her treats or anything to get her to like me. She just accepts me. Dogs are all right, I guess.

We walk in silence for another block. Checking the next location on the list, I nearly crack a smile. I'm not sure why M had me visit Walls and then sent me marching off to James Sidney Hinton Park, but it's all the excuse I need to head back over there. I feel like I'm collecting dots I haven't connected yet. Walls is a piece of work, building stuff no one asked for. Judging from his clothes, he seems to be doing all right for a business with few customers. I guess I also don't mind the company.

I'm pretty sure Thmei stops to pee near every third bush. It makes the walk over to Crown Hill take that much longer. UNWA is actually several neighborhoods clustered under the same umbrella, all trying to not get wet. Riverside on the south, United Northwest in the middle (tucked alongside Golden

Hill), and Crown Hill on the north. It's all The Land to me, but it's not a short walk.

"You ever been to James Sidney Hinton Park?" I ask.

"No. Parks ain't my thing."

"What, you were born grown?"

"It ain't that." Aaries's face twists a bit, a wince he tries to hide. "I'm kinda new to the neighborhood."

"You staying at Ms. Campbell's."

"Yeah. Finally got settled in."

"What's that about?"

"I . . ." Aaries stares straight ahead, and shifts like his skin suddenly doesn't fit right. "I had to leave my place. Since I got a background, I'm still on papers for some stupid stuff I got into—and my PO said I had to have a place to stay so M let me crash with him until he got me connected with Ms. Campbell. I help him out with chores, errands, and stuff. Paint the porch. Redo the floors. Projects he can't do anymore."

"So, you more like Alfred than Robin."

He smiles weakly, so I decide to give him some space.

We walk so far into the east side of the neighborhood I can see the gates of Crown Hill Cemetery on the other side of Doctor M.L.K. Jr Street. The roar of traffic fills my ears as we near the I-65 overpass. The highway winds through the neighborhood, dividing it up so that certain blocks exist in their own pocket universes.

People can't travel from one part of The Land to the next except along Clifton or 30th Street. Or crossing the pedestrian bridge on 35th Street that runs over the highway, if that person doesn't mind the forest of poison ivy growing all around.

"To hear my mom tell it, when they started building the highway back in the sixties, the government got to scooping up people's houses like they were Halloween candy." It always frustrated my mom. That feeling of powerlessness overwhelmed her to the point where she couldn't do anything. I feel her. I bet this is why my associates at school call me too serious all the time.

"Things ain't changed that much. It's one reason UNWA formed in the first place, to organize neighbors." He gets that uncomfortable sound in his voice again. "Always something dividing folks."

The sidewalk crumbles into a sea of rocks as the lone alleyway cuts off. I can barely see the path we're supposed to be following. I have to brush aside the limbs of overgrown bushes like I'm on a safari. The branches barely leave enough room to walk before shoving me into the grass. I stumble onto a sign almost by accident.

JAMES SIDNEY HINTON PARK
"Envisioned by Neighbors Helping Neighbors"

A nearby plaque tells James Sidney Hinton's story. He was the first African American to hold office in the state legislature in Indiana. Slowly I turn around, trying to find the legacy built in this man's honor.

"What. The entire heck. Am I looking at?" The words trip out my mouth and I'm glad no one can hear what I really think.

"I think someone forgot what they were supposed to be building," Aaries says.

A series of wood pylons, like stumps sawed off at random angles, marks the border of the park. And I'm not gonna lie: "park" is a strong word to describe the place. More like a grass lot with a hill in the middle of it. Three recently constructed houses line the other side of the field. Not too far from me, a single basketball hoop stands like an unwanted weed. More like just the frame of one—little more than a rim on a pole—since there's no backboard. Or net. Or surface to play on other than grass, which isn't exactly great for dribbling a ball. Like someone just bought the stuff from Sam's Club and forgot to finish putting it together.

We walk toward the back of the park, where someone has piled dirt into a mound. The front of the hill has tires sticking out of it, stacked and arranged along its face like a rubber cliff. Large rocks circle the hill. I don't know if this is supposed to be someone's idea of modern art, but I know art, and this ain't it. Behind it, a fence separates the park from the embankment leading to the highway. On the other side of the mound, someone has started to build a slide and swing set combo. But it's been abandoned, unfinished.

"How does everything here seem new and worn-out at the same time?" Aaries runs his hand through the wood chips beneath the playground.

I have the unshakable feeling someone boosted

them from another park. Thmei rolls around in the chips anyway.

"Check this out." Screws pop out an inch or so from the playground set as if someone couldn't be bothered to make them flush against the surface. "It's like someone used old wood to try to build a new jungle gym, then came back months later with some used screws."

"I wonder what idiot came up with this," Aaries says.

"You mean a park that doesn't fit and that no one asked for?" I scoff. "A community garden would at least serve a function."

I check the charge on my phone. It's down to 20 percent but has enough battery to document some of this. I film the basketball post and get close-ups of the swing set with all its loose screws. When my power dips to 10 percent, I switch to camera mode to snap a few pics of the exposed nails. I train the camera toward the three houses at the end of the lot; one of the back doors swing open. I tuck my phone into my pocket and dive out of sight behind a row of bushes. Aaries doesn't even check behind him—as soon as I duck, he automatically hides. Rushing over to me, Thmei whines softly, confused by our game. I stroke her head to keep her from barking.

I pop my head up enough to see none other than Mattea shuffle out onto her back porch. I point in her direction. Aaries nods and army-crawls toward me, staying out of sight. That boy does too much. She's not exactly the SWAT team. Without her fancy going-to-a-meeting clothes and hat as her armor, she looks like any other frail elderly woman. Although she doesn't have her cane, she clutches her cell phone like a scared old white lady. Probably has 911 already punched in.

It's a public park, so I'm not trespassing, but I don't need her knowing I'm snooping around. Shrinking lower against the bush, I wait as Mattea inspects first her backyard and then does a visual sweep of the park. Satisfied that no one's around, she hops into her car. Her license plate reads, "MS. ODOM." I wait a full thirty seconds after she drives off before sneaking out.

Because I can't help myself, I leave Aaries in the bushes and creep up to her house to peek inside. Mattea isn't on M's list, but she's definitely on mine.

The rooms are barely decorated. No photos or art on the walls. The shelves have no knickknacks.

Slinking around to the kitchen, I see there's not a dish out, not even in the sink.

When I turn back to the park, I get mad. This hot mess is insulting. To me. To my community. To James Sidney Hinton.

"I've seen enough," I announce.

"What are you going to do?"

"What makes you think I'm going to do anything?"

"You got that *I got a bad idea* energy all over your face." Aaries shrugs.

"You must be confusing that with my *I'm hungry and I'm going to find something to eat* face. Catch you later? I can swing by M's and we can finish off the list."

Aaries studies me. I knew acting too nice might be pushing it. "Whatever. You do you."

He takes Thmei's leash and heads back toward Clifton. I act like I'm heading north until they fall out of sight, then double back toward Mattea's place. I know she's hiding something.

Checking back over my shoulder, I reach into my bag. I spread out my paint cans like surgical instruments on a tray. With black, I begin to outline a tag on the wall of Mattea's house that's visible to passing traffic. I pick up can after can, fleshing out the image of a park on fire. Ten minutes later, I wipe away the sheen of sweat from my forehead and step back to appreciate my handiwork. I'm ready to sign it when red and blue lights erupt all around me.

"I'M GOING TO need you to sit down." The officer raises his voice at me like I didn't hear him the first time. Clearly I'm ignoring him. Even though he's busted me before, I can't take him seriously with that stupid patch of squirrel fur along his upper lip wriggling when he talks. He towers over me, trying to use his height to intimidate. Two things work against him. One, I'm in middle school. *Almost* every adult towers over me, so it's just another day that ends in Y. Two, I've had to sit across from my school principal, Mrs. Fitzgerald. That woman has laser eyes and a resting gangsta face. After her, no adult scares me.

I post up on a stretch of curb. The squad cars' lights reflect on my face, blinding me every so often.

He calls in a female officer to make sure things don't look funny. The flashing lights, the police, people hovering around: they remind me of the night they took Mom away.

"There's nothing in here that will stick me is there?" His voice thick and flat with condescension, the male officer snaps on latex gloves to go through my backpack.

"I'm not a junkie," I tell him.

The officer makes a derisive snort. Police assume everyone in The Land is a junkie. He piles my change of clothes in the grass, alongside my sketch pad, clipboard, and spray cans. A freezer bag holds my toiletries. He dangles it in front of me, maybe wanting to shame me, but I just stare at him. Again, I'm in middle school. I refuse to give a bully any power over me. Not knowing what else to do, I begin to reach for my sketch pad. I slow down to assure the officer that I'm not reaching for anything more dangerous than paper. And so there's no confusion, I fish a Willow charcoal stick from the pile, nothing to be confused with a possible weapon.

I know I'm getting anxious, so I begin drawing to control my feelings. This situation's big enough.

I have priors with this cop and he's not inclined to show me any favors. I scan the nearby bushes and houses, calculating my chances of making a break for it, when I hear tires squeal to a halt.

"Why don't we leave the young lady's stuff alone." M steps out of the passenger side of an old beat-up red truck. Aaries hops out the driver's side, his business face on as he shadows M. Not bothering to close the door behind him, M hobbles with a slight stiff-legged limp. Despite his wobble, with his red leather fedora low on his head, the way he moves toward us like a red-capped shark is almost gangsta.

The officer sets my bag down and moves to intercept M, his hand drifting down to his holster. M extends his hands out by his waist, his long spidery fingers spread wide apart. "I can't see too good. Is your hand going for your gun?"

"Just a precaution, sir." The officer glances back at his partner. She takes a single step away from me, keeping both me and M in her sights. Her hands are nowhere near her weapon, though. Only a raised hand to signal me to stay still.

"I get it, I get it. An old man sneaking up on an

armed officer half his age may be perceived as threatening to said officer. Make that officer fear for his safety, and we know how that story ends." M holds his arms up in a *don't shoot me* gesture. "What seems to be the problem?"

"Young lady here was caught vandalizing private property." The officer pats the air for M to lower his hands.

"Was she now?" M turns my way, his eyes not fixing on me in particular.

I glance at Aaries. Though he doesn't take his eyes off the officer, especially his gun, he half shrugs enough for me to see. He must've not been as out of sight as I thought when I went to tag Mattea's house.

"We are detaining her and investigating for trespass, among other things."

"I get it, I get it. You have to ascertain who she is and such." Waving for Aaries to come around the truck, M raises his voice. "I'm having my associate, Aaries Greyer, come over. That's a phone in his hand. He's walking slowly, hands in plain sight, not a threat to anyone, but he is filming this."

Aaries eases toward us slowly, one hand raised,

the other clutching his cell phone carefully in front of his face. A coordinated show that they'd obviously performed before.

"Sir, I'm going to need you to step back." The officer is getting frustrated. M's presence disrupts his control over the scene. "Right now, you're dangerously close to obstructing an officer during the course of his duties. That's a jailable offense."

"Well, we wouldn't want that." M's fingers ball into a fist, which he raises. Aaries stops dead in his tracks but keeps filming. "Would it speed things along to say she was with me?"

"And who might you be?"

"Menelik Paschall."

Recognizing the name, the two officers glance at each other. Their expressions say this is a headache well above their pay grades.

"We're going to check with the property owner to see how she wants to proceed." The officer backs away to knock on the door while his partner watches us. Tapping me on the shoulder, she lets me move to M's side.

"Your name must really ring out," I whisper. "You got police on pause."

"You know my family has a long, complicated relationship with law enforcement."

I finish my first sketch, of a scaly beast stared down by an old wizard.

Not too long after my dad . . . left us, I got in trouble for being disruptive in class. Teachers accused me of talking back, distracting those around me, and not doing my work. Since I was half Black, the white kids kept poking me and poking me until I snapped at them, yelling that I just wanted to be left alone. My mom got called to Mrs. Fitzgerald's office and wasn't happy about it. She was mad she had to take off work. It was time off she couldn't afford, not with us having no idea how we were going to make bills. While we waited outside the principal's office, I confessed to my mom everything that had been going on, something shifted in her. Mom marched into Mrs. Fitzgerald's office and raged until Mrs. Fitzgerald saw me—*truly* saw me—and what I'd been going through. My main memory is loving my mother in that moment. Because she went to war for me.

There's just something real about someone willing to fight for you.

The spitting of pebbles under tires snaps me out

of my thoughts. That and a shrill voice.

"That you, M?" Mattea climbs out of her car. There's nothing frail about her now.

"Oh Lord." It's M's turn to be thrown off his game. He lowers his voice, "I was hoping we could've got ghost before we had to deal with her."

"Hey, I'm ready to leave whenever you are," I say.

"What brings you out?" Mattea reaches out both her hands and engulfs one of his, the way the jaws of a trap snap shut.

"Heard a friend had stepped in it. Thought I'd see what was up." M slips his hand free from hers and wipes his pant leg.

"Meddling. As always." Mattea ignores the motion, and though she circles the both of us, she's really studying me. Trying to figure out how me and M know each other. What we're up to. That same look teachers get when they know someone's been clowning and are trying to narrow down their pool of suspects. "I recognize her. The way she butted in at the meeting, I should have known she was with you, M." Her eyes lock on mine. "You spray-paint my place?"

"Don't answer that." M's voice has a note of caution in it.

"You her lawyer, too?" Mattea side-eyes him.

"Yes." He gives me a sharp nod. "I'm also speaking as a concerned party. She's a good kid. An honor student. Neither one of us wants another young Black child, full of potential, to get unnecessarily caught up in the system."

"True that." Mattea softens. She nods the male officer over.

"Ma'am?" the officer asks.

"It's all right. Just a misunderstanding between friends. We good here." She doesn't take her eyes off M.

"Ma'am." The officer half bows, practically tipping his hat to her, but glares at M, mean mugging him all the way back to his car.

"Always making friends wherever you go. You enjoy certain perks from the family business," Mattea continues.

"I have nothing to do with my family." M spits off to the side.

"Please, you every bit as gangsta. You send her to tag my house? Send me a message?"

"She . . . took initiative." M glances at me, silently scolding.

97

"Well, your dog's off her leash. Get her back on before she finds herself put down."

"Hey . . ." I whirl toward her. My hand balls into a fist around my charcoal stick.

M rests a hand on my shoulder to settle me down. "We can call it a misunderstanding."

"She repaints my house and we'll consider it community service. Time served." Mattea begins to walk away but stops short with an additional thought. She raises a finger. "And . . ."

"And?" M arches a wary eyebrow.

She levels her eyes at him like laser sights. "You'll owe me a favor."

M hesitates. He's careful with his next words. "You know how I roll."

"It won't hurt the community," she assures him.

"A favor, then," he says slowly, with a hint of sadness.

This is my mess. What have I just dragged M into?

11

"**WELL, THAT WAS** an interesting first day," M says once we're in the truck.

Aaries opens the other side to slide into the driver's seat. The engine sputters when he turns the key. He catches my eye, not showing any embarrassment when the truck doesn't start.

"You sure you allowed to drive? As a sophomore?" I ask.

"I got my permit. Before you say anything slick, I got held back a year."

"Aaries has what I call . . . an adversarial relationship with school," M says.

"That sounds like all of my relationships," I say.

M laughs, a heavy thing that starts deep in his gut. "I bet it does."

Cranking the engine one more time, Aaries stomps the gas pedal until something under the hood snags and coughs itself to life. A needle on the dashboard swerves far to the right. The windshield wipers for no reason flail once, waving hello, and the truck idles its way down the alley out of sight of the park, the police, and, most important, Mattea.

"Look, I admit I got heated. I had to do something," I blurt out.

"Did I ask about that? I ain't mad. Maybe a little disappointed." M allows a heartbeat or two for the words to settle in before his mouth broadens into a mischievous grin. "Girl, you ain't always got to put your game out front. You have to be strategic with your actions. Might as well put up a billboard that says, 'We suspicious of you.' Mattea's on guard now. So what does that tell you?"

M's reaction knocks me off-balance. I was still preparing a whole speech defending myself. It takes me a moment to shift and actually consider his question. "That I can't come at her direct anymore."

"True. Or if you do, you better have overwhelming

force. If you go for the queen, you better take out the queen."

"My bad."

"For what? We all just out here learning." M twists back around in his seat, the streetlights reflecting from his frosted eyes. "Anyone try to make a bad sale to you today?"

I make a noncommitted noise as I think about Clarence Walls. I don't know what to do with that. Opening my pack, I rummage through it in a bit of a show. "They never gave me back my paint."

"Well, you *were* committing a crime." A lot of the play leaves M's voice. "Let's not lose sight of that."

"You gonna get on me about that?" Clutching my violated backpack to my chest, I cross my arms. I brace myself for another adult ready to come down on me.

"Not at all." M pauses like he's keeping a sigh out of his voice. "Just pointing out why they took your spray cans. Keep in mind, that's all they did. It could have been worse."

"It was enough." I slump in the back seat and fold my arms tighter. "The favor Mattea mentioned. Is that . . . will that cost you a lot?"

"It might." M doesn't even try to dance around the fact.

I feel respected on one hand; on the other, I still feel some sort of way. He's in debt because of me. Which means that I owe him, and I hate that. I shouldn't be letting myself get close to him, especially since I've already disappointed him.

It's only a matter of time before he leaves me behind, too.

We come up to the intersection behind Clifton Corner where the Village Bodega is. It's part convenience store, part farmers market, all run as a nonprofit. A sign in the window reads, "Going Out of Business."

"I want some Oreos. Can you get me some?" My mind begins its usual calculations, plotting a route of leaving him before he leaves me. The way my dad did.

One time when Dad and I got home, the house was a complete wreck. Couch cushions tossed aside. All the drawers and cabinets open. A box of cereal emptied out on the counter. We found Mom huddled in a corner, her eyes darting all over the place.

Confused, like she didn't recognize us. Then she got
suspicious of us, her attention focused on me.

"Where'd you hide it?"

"Hide what?" Tears welled up in my eyes as
soon as she accused me. Like I was already guilty
of doing whatever she thought I did. Dad stepped
between us.

"My necklace. I know you took it."

Dad reached out to hold her shoulders, but she
shrugged him off. His tone was low and calm, never
angry. Almost sad. "Honey, you threw it away. You
threw all your jewelry away."

Mom tilted her head to the side. After a few
seconds, her eyes brightened like she recognized me.
"That's right."

"Go on to your room and get started on your
homework," Dad said.

"No, wait," Mom said. "I didn't mean to scare
you. I just get lost in my thoughts sometimes. You
know how you wake up suddenly from a dream and
for a minute you might get confused about what's
real and what's not?"

I stare at her, not knowing what she really
wanted. Something about her was so off.

"The voices . . . ," Mom continued, but Dad coughed, cutting her off.

"You know what I'm never confused by?" Mom made her thumbs-up sign and waited.

I stared at her thumb like it was a trap ready to spring shut. Mom's eyes begged me to mirror her. I did, but even as I said the words, "My heart," they were an empty promise.

I went to my room. Kinda numb. I wanted to cry. We never talked about it. Not really. Not even after Dad left. That was when the anger started living in me.

"Sure." M tugs out his wallet. His fingers peel back the bills until he reaches a ten and hands it to me. "It's been a long day. I might as well reward inventive thinking and action."

I grab for the bill. M clutches onto it just for a heartbeat, staring at me with intent, like he knows what I'm thinking, before he lets it go.

I bound out of the truck as soon as it slows to a stop. A sign on the store window announces that it's closing soon due to rezoning. Another thing preparing to leave me. When I come out of the store, I pile into the back seat and hand back two dollars. M holds the bills up, Aaries says "ones," and M folds the corner in a pattern before slipping them back into his wallet.

M waits a few seconds. Aaries glances at him but doesn't drive off.

"Those were some expensive cookies," M says finally.

"I gave you change," I protest.

"Those were some eight-dollar Oreos?"

I'd bought a package on sale for $2.25. I snatch out the remaining bills and thrust them toward him. "If you want all your change back, here, take it."

"It ain't about the change. It's about you trying to be slick with it." M raises his hand up like a stop sign. "I don't need the money back. If you need it, just say you need it. It's all good. Just don't try to run game on me."

The air becomes hot. It's hard to breathe. All I can hear are the voices of people who entered and abruptly left my life. I know better than to allow people to get close to me. That isn't safe.

"I don't need it. I don't need you." I open my door and slam it behind me. I lug my backpack high onto my shoulder and storm off into the night. My phone rings. I stare at the caller ID. It's M. Glaring back toward them, I make a show of declining the call.

I said that I'm an exit specialist. It's a gift from my parents. I learned from the best.

Aaries and M drive off.

THE NEXT DAY, the sunlight slaps me in the face to wake me up. I check my phone. Down to 5 percent. I change, watching some of the video I recorded of the park. My clothes spill out of the nearest garbage bag. When I moved out, I had piled everything I owned into the bags and carted them over to the Ryder house. I'll have to do a laundry run before too long. The laundromat is just up on 38th Street but it's such a chore lugging everything back and forth. It's one reason I tend to let things stack up, even if that only makes doing laundry more difficult in the end.

My belly grumbles.

Reaching into my bag, I dig out the pack of

Oreos. Last night when I got back to the Ryder house I couldn't bring myself to eat any of them. Shoveling a couple into my mouth now, they still kind of taste like ashes. It was only five dollars. M didn't have to make such a big deal of things.

Neither did you, a small part within me whispers. But I never trust voices in my head, especially when they sound like my own. I squash that noise down deep, along with any other thought trying to point out that I picked a random fight with M over nothing so that I would have an excuse to leave him before it occurred to him to abandon me.

But now I have no way of getting money.

"Hold up," I shout, and snap my fingers. I turn to my jazz council: the statues of Sarah, Wes, and Grover. Okay, I get that my talking to them may be a little weird. I'm the same way at school. I avoid people my own age. Some of my associates make fun of me for acting too white. Others think I'm too Black. So I end up not talking to many folks. My jazz council may be a little less conversational, but they give me room to think out loud. "M never paid me."

I wait on M's front porch for nearly five minutes before I commit to pounding on it like police with a warrant. My first knocks are met with a flurry of barks and a whirl of claws against wood floor. The sudden thump and then pause in the scraping tells me that Thmei doesn't round the corner well and slides into the table before regaining her footing. The dog barks and scratches from the other side of the door until the booming thuds of Aaries's heavy footfalls follow. He opens the door but only enough to show his face.

"I know you saw me out here." I cross my arms in defiance. "What took you so long to answer?"

"What took you so long to knock?" Aaries stares me down. The door doesn't open any farther.

"I was deciding."

"So were we." Aaries budges only as much as I do. He almost sounds in his feelings about me bouncing on them.

I hate that they have the upper hand. My tone lightens but only a hair. "What'd you decide?"

"I answered, didn't I? What do you want?"

"To see the old man." If there was any certainty in my voice, it's run off to hide. I talk to the ground while I keep making my case. "He owes me money."

"Does he now?" Aaries opens the door a little more to slouch against the frame, amused. He doesn't know he's playing with fire right now.

"We had an agreement. I did my job."

"You also went off script."

"Technically the job got done first. He available or not?" I let my hands relax, since I notice I had clenched my fists. "You don't have to keep playing games if you're not going to let me in."

"All right." Aaries turns around to leave but leaves the door open for me. He leads me back to M's office.

I'm still not sold on whatever M thought he was trying to teach me. But if I want to figure out what Mattea is hiding, much less find resources for a mural project, I need real help.

"What's this I hear about me owing someone some money?" M spins around in his chair, bridging his fingers in front of him like an overdramatic super-villain. "I guess keeping folks out of jail ain't good enough for a day's work. They gonna make me put in some overtime."

"I just wanted to—" I stop short. I'm careful not to meet his eyes because a part of me is scared that I'll see something angry or accusing. I didn't come here to say I'm sorry, but my voice falters a bit, nearly breaking with something close to apology. "Collect the money I was due."

"That it?" M's face screws up like he's covering his skepticism.

It gets on my nerves the way he manages to look at me like he's seen my act before. "That's it."

"How much I owe?"

"You said ten dollars an hour. Four hours solid." I think about trying to squeeze a full eight-hour day out of him for my efforts, but that ashy taste fills my mouth again.

"So, if we say forty, that make us good?"

"Yeah."

Aaries comes around with an envelope and hands it to me.

I open it and count. "There's eighty dollars."

"You put in a full day. Even showed some initiative. Things didn't quite work out the way you intended, but we're all still here to fight another day. Besides, your bit of initiative cost you your paints. And you'll have to buy some to fix the damage you did. Figured least I could do was help with that."

Our business concluded, M turns back around to

his monitors. He scrolls through articles. Facebook posts. Nextdoor boards. Keeping up with the news and gossip within the community. Though he stops talking to me, I don't feel like he's dismissed me yet.

"Can you even read any of that?" I ask.

"My eyes ain't all bad. Besides, I have Aaries read things to me when things get tough."

Aaries leashes Thmei to take her for a walk. It's like they're leaving the next move up to me. The peal of a trumpet to some sort of march music snags my attention.

"You listening to the frog choker again." I settle onto the couch and start charging my phone.

"*Sketches of Spain* is my second favorite Miles Davis album." M doesn't turn around, his fingers not skipping a beat.

"What's your first?"

"*Kind of Blue.* We can listen to it some other time. This one helps me think through problems." M closes his eyes. His thumb and forefinger connect like he's pinching something I can't see. Slowly he begins conducting. His head sways back and forth, caught up in the play, riding the notes. It's almost hypnotic watching him.

"My dad"—I hesitate at the thought of him—
"used to listen to Charles Mingus a lot."

"That so? He's good, too." M turns to face me,
his expression not unkind. "You know what you can
learn from jazz? How to improvise. You gather your
team, learn what they can do, and when one of you
goes off script, everyone trusts each other to just
move in their flow."

After a while, I slide down the couch closer to
him, that way I can watch without disturbing him. M
snaps back awake to study his array of monitors. He
skims through social media, credit reports, financial
papers, working his way down a list I hadn't noticed
before, written in the kind of scrawl a five-year-old
might make.

"What are you doing?" I squint at his screens.

"Let's call it opposition research. You have to
know who you're up against. Do your homework to
figure out who their friends are. That's how you get
the lay of the land so that you can figure out the best
course forward."

"I don't have any opposition."

"If you don't have opposition, you aren't doing
much. And it pushes you to develop."

"Looks like you're 'developing' all up in their business." I lean closer as the information scrolls by. "Can you, uh, look up *anything*?"

"Not anything, but there's a whole lot of collected public information out there if you know where to look. Facebook alone is a treasure trove. You have to remember that you always leave traces of yourself online and someone's always watching."

"Someone like you."

"I'm harmless. A gnat." M turns around to me with his mischievous grin in place. "Why do you ask?"

"Could you look up stuff about me? Or my parents?"

"I could." M holds his hands out, palms up. I don't know how to react. He simply continues to keep them out. Waiting. I tentatively touch one, flinching as if it might be a trap, before resting my hands in his. He closes his long fingers around my hand, gently. "Miss Bella 'Unfadeable' Fades, I promise not to dig into you or your life without your permission. I'll only know what you tell me. Fair?"

"Fair." I take my hands back and he goes back to his business. I glance at his list. I see Mattea's name on it. And Walls's. "How are all these people connected?"

"You can't fight a system unless you understand how it works. It's like I tried telling Aaries before I helped him withdraw from his school and transfer to an internet one. He was going to war with all of his teachers. One after another, just a hardheaded approach. What he needed were more finesse and strategy."

"I'm assuming you're not pushing that I drop out of school."

"Not quite." He hands me an invitation. "How would you like to go to a party to do some next-level opposition research?"

I grin. "Will there be free food?"

13

"**AM I DRESSED** okay?" I extend my arms like a ballerina about to spin, all to show off my blouse and blue skirt outfit. They'd been buried at the bottom of my clothes bag back at Mr. Ryder's house. I don't have a lot of occasions to dress up.

"You might be asking the wrong person. They're lucky I even bothered with a buttoned-up shirt and matching pants." M's limp has him tottering from side to side more than usual as he walks over to join me at the mirror. "I'm an old dusty something who doesn't give a . . . anything what people think of him. They invited me, they get me. As is."

"Yeah, well, *I* still don't want to be underdressed."

I hate the idea that my clothes might embarrass M. Since we're only barely back on good terms.

"They're going to judge us no matter what we wear. You have to figure out how to navigate that," M says. I think he wants people to underestimate him. He likes it when people guess wrong about him.

"You look fine," Aaries says as he comes around the corner. Cool without trying, he's in a royal-blue collared shirt, unbuttoned at the top. The color is good against his dark skin. His pants are casual, not dressy.

They're both comfortable with who they are, so the clothes don't matter. For some reason, this makes me relax.

"There you go," M says. "The people whose opinions matter think you look fine."

"You don't count. You half blind," Aaries says.

"I still see better than most." M winks.

～

The Columbia Club is a private spot on Monument Circle. It wouldn't surprise me if all the families who live in Golden Hill are members there. It's the player place to be if you're in business—any kind of business. But only the big ballers in Indianapolis could show up here. The building looks like a cross between an old church and a hotel, with arched windows that bulge from the walls and pictures carved into the limestone. Like they want to impress people with the appearance of that fresh-off-the-Mayflower money.

"On my best day, I could never get in a place like this," I say when M takes my hand to steady himself as we exit the truck. Aaries turns the keys over to the valet attendant and watches uneasily as the truck leaves his sight.

"Well, we ain't in yet." M escorts me along the carpet under the signature red awning leading to the front door of the club.

"May I help you?" a red-faced white dude says in a tone meant to stop us cold. His thin mustache runs down his chin to join a thin beard that just outlines his face. His black T-shirt is purposely a size too small to show off his muscles.

"We here for the party." M's tone can't be taken seriously. It's all a silly game to him.

The man takes a long snide up-and-down study of M, from his red leather fedora to his wrinkled shirt.

"Wheeler Mission is farther down on Market Street. There's no 'party' here. You must be mistaken."

"Maybe. Wouldn't be the first time." M about-faces to leave. Aaries doesn't miss a step, as if he'd seen this play before, so I quickly fall in behind them. With his back to the man, M calls out, "I guess my old friend Blake Harrison gave me the wrong address."

"Hold on." The man's voice constricts, and when I glance back, his ruddy face blanches all shades of pale. "*You're* a friend of Mr. Harrison's?"

"Didn't I mention that?" M keeps his back to the man but aims a coy smile my way.

"Do you have an invitation?" No hiding his skepticism; the man's tone tinges with uncertainty.

"Aaries, could you hand him my invitation?"

Aaries slips the doorman an envelope. The man reads it with ever-widening eyes.

"Well," he says finally, "this allows only a plus one."

"Here she is." M thrusts his elbow out. Not knowing what's expected of me, I awkwardly half curtsy. M chokes back a laugh, pretending that he has a sudden cough. Eventually, I recognize my cue and take his arm.

"What about him?" The man nods his chin toward Aaries.

"I'm all but blind. He's my eyes."

"I can't let him in."

"Aaries, can you retrieve my invitation from the man? We can give Blake my regards some other time."

"Wait." The man eyes us nervously. "I can make this one exception."

"Thank you," M says.

We follow the signs to the Imagine Indy Project banquet. The hall's a shadowed cavern that opens up into a brightly lit room. Cloth napkins folded like birds decorate each table. They got more forks, knives, and spoons beside each plate than I've ever seen. Servers in red jackets line the walls like prison guards, rotating out who wanders the floor with trays of snacks. The guests mill about in fancy dresses and hand-tailored suits and tuxedos. A jazz quartet sits in the corner. I recognize their piece from the frog choker's album.

"Who's Blake Harrison?"

"He runs CISC. They're going to be dividing out two hundred and fifty thousand dollars to a few groups soon, which has everyone foaming like dogs in heat."

"I don't think that's how dogs work," I say.

"Whatever. You know what I mean." M waves me off. "I'm sure he's around here somewhere. He's the man people wait for and the name to drop because everyone worries about possibly offending him. Almost everyone."

"Wait, so are we going to ask CISC for money directly?"

"Not quite. We're here to see who all's here asking."

"That makes no sense."

"Oh, I know. But when big money's involved, there are certain ways people go about asking for it. Like throwing a party for the people who want to give them money."

"Big money like an extra one hundred K for a park?"

"Now you're getting it."

I shrug because the ways money and politics work still make no sense. "You didn't have to flex on the bouncer dude back there," I whisper.

"But where's the fun in that?" M hums to himself, his head bobbing as he strides through the room. All that's missing is a cane for the little strut that he's doing.

I notice all of the attention that focuses on M that he probably can't see. I say "probably" because I have the unshakable feeling that playing up his poor eyesight is another one of his tricks to throw people off. That thing that magicians do. Misdirection. And he loves to bathe in the weird energy of people being mad he's in the room. Like it's his personal hater's ball.

There's something else going on with me. I realize that I'm at a fancy party with folk who control the money and power: politicians, businesspeople, the real movers and shakers in the city all gathered. Everything feels so . . . big. And I'm here. Even if I'm not dressed as elegant as them. I never dreamed that I'd be at something like this. It's like it wakes a part of me, like I'm supposed to feel really pretty. Gawking at the pageantry and production, all the beautiful and powerful people gathered, I can't help but feel like I'm out of my depth.

"I don't belong here." I cross my arms in front of

me in an attempt to cover my outfit.

"No one does. But we're here to observe all of the power players in the city in their natural environment."

"There ain't nothing natural about any of this."

"Do you know why I brought you here?" M asks.

"You said to see the players."

"That's part of it."

"Free food?"

"That's also part of it. I'll always eat on someone else's dime."

"Then what?"

"So you can see the whole system. What you're really up against." M thumbs toward Aaries. "You remember what I was saying about pulling Aaries out of school because of his attitude toward his teachers?"

"They were dumb," Aaries mutters.

"All of them, huh?" M cuts his eyes toward him.

"All of them."

"Well, I laid it out for him. One or two teachers he might be able to be mad at, not play their games. But he didn't have the resources to fight a war on every front. No one does. You have to pick your targets."

"They're just teachers, not Navy Seals," I said.

"That's what I was saying," Aaries said.

"But it's also the administration. The principal, vice principal, deans. Other kids' parents. The rules. The school board. An entire system. And you're just one student. You have to see all the pieces to see who has the power. They are your leverage points."

"What's that got to do with this room?" I ask.

"This is the system. On display with hors d'oeuvres. They the money people. The lawmakers. The gatekeepers. Who do you see too few of?"

I scan the room, not seeing many faces like mine. "The community."

"Now you getting it."

The Columbia Club crowd reminds me of some of the kids at Persons Crossings Public Academy who make jokes they think are funny but are actually insulting. No matter how polite they seem, there's something scary underneath. And it's hungry.

That's when I see them on the other side of the room. Fury and Jared.

FURY AND JARED don't see me. Yet. Meanwhile, they're looking every bit as uncomfortable as I feel.

"Hey, I'm going to scout around on my own a bit."

"Remember, if you meet someone you don't know, make sure to introduce yourself. Never be afraid to—"

"Let people know who I am. I know."

M runs his fingers through his scraggly beard. "And bring me back a plate of anything that looks interesting."

Keeping my eyes on the boys, I stroll around the room. At first I think they don't recognize me because I'm out of context. The way that I'm used to seeing my teachers at school, but if I bump into them at the grocery store in jeans and a ratty T-shirt, it's gonna take me a minute. Still, ain't but a dozen Black faces in this whole place, including them, me, M, and Aaries. (I mean, I get that me and M are pretty light-skinned, but we still obviously Black.)

Then the music turns up a little louder. The jazz quartet playing in the corner goes all in, trying to play a Lizzo song. I just can't with them right now. It's a crime against music. I liked it better when they stayed in their lane with the frog choker's stuff. Then a true crime against humanity happens: Mattea takes the dance floor.

I can't look away.

Mattea's cutting it up out there. Actually, she's not bad and not just for someone's grandma. More like she might have been a bad girl back in her day. Clarence Walls is out there, too, flailing about like he's being tased during a perp walk. Slipping my phone out, I record for a bit. This has to be preserved.

When I've recorded enough, I search for Fury and Jared. I can't find them at first, but when I turn to head back to M, there they are. Cutting me off from him. For a heartbeat, I worry but this party is like sacred ground. They ain't gonna do no hood mess up in here. Especially when it looks like every other person is an undercover cop.

"What you two doing here?" I ask.

"Well, well, well. Lookie here, lookie here." Jared leers at me. He looks like Christmas exploded all over him. A white shirt with a weird swirl of green and red prints. Red jeans. Red high-top Converse with a custom paint job that matches his shirt. He should've stole Fury's whole drip.

"Looks like we have a lost sheep," Fury says.

I ain't gonna lie: Fury cleans up nice. I ain't out here trying to catch feelings for some boy. This is all strictly casual observation because, you know, God gave me eyes. A black button-down shirt with jeans. A print of a stylized gold dragon on the left shoulder spilling onto his chest.

I mean, if you're gonna vaguely threaten someone, at least look cute doing it.

A server comes by with a tray loaded with food. There's a plate of tomatoes and mozzarella on skewers (pass). Lamb chops. Chicken drums drizzled in a brown sauce. Pastry stuffed with creamy spinach. Some sort of spiced diced tomatoes on toasted bread (also pass).

We all glance at each other and then at the food, declaring a silent truce.

"How you even get through the door?" I pile a few lamb chops on a plate. They're cut up into individual bones, making it so that a person has to work to get full up in there.

"Clarence Walls." With a shrug, Fury samples all of the hors d'oeuvres. He eyes me warily, but he's not going to let my presence interrupt food that's free. "His . . . mentorship program."

"Mentorship, huh?" Despite my initial judgment, I try the tomato-and-cheese skewer. I should have trusted my instincts. Straight-up trash, but I make myself finish it. I can't bring myself to waste food.

"He made a deal with our boss." Jared snatches chicken off the tray and gnaws it down to the bone in three sloppy bites. He tries to set it back on the server's tray, but the man swerves the food away and jerks his head toward a stack of empty plates. "Running errands for Walls and the pastor makes us look respectable."

Fury glares at Jared so hard, he nearly drops his chicken.

I grow uncomfortable with the silence growing

128

between them. I've overheard something I shouldn't. Their boss. He means Pass. They're still Paschall Crew, but Walls has a deal with him. That's a cozy arrangement I bet no one wants to get out. I file the information away for later. Jared remains oblivious, but Fury studies me, calculating how big a threat I am. I play things off as best I can. "I guess children are the future and all."

"I see you still got a smart mouth," Jared says.

"I see you still getting dressed in the dark." Lost in the moment, I grab a few more lamb chops from another passing server for my walking-around plate. Out of reflex, I escalate. "Nice shoes."

Jared's eyes bug out. There's an actual sting of pain beneath his expression. I wonder if he painted those shoes himself. And was proud of them.

That thought makes me feel kinda bad.

Jared steps toward me like he wants to do something, but Fury stops him with a hand to the chest. Fury turns to me with his slow heavy gaze. "You know, you won't always be here. Safe. We'll see you again. Out there."

"Where she'll be fine." Aaries had approached without me noticing.

"Long time, cuzzin." Fury takes note of him, unmoved.

"Long time." They dap each other up, but it's a cold thing. Out of respect or obligation, not because they like each other.

"She with you?"

"*We* with M." Aaries lays the words out real slow. "You both remember M, right?"

I don't understand the look that passes between them. The shared history of Fury and Aaries. The history of M and these boys. All I know is that the moment is heavy.

"It's like that?" Fury asks.

"It's like that. We good?" Aaries lets the question hang there.

"For now." Fury, followed by Jared, moves out of our way.

"Come on." Aaries turns to me while we keep walking. "M's been wondering where you are."

We wander up to M. Just as we get there, a waiter passes by with a tray full of glasses filled with something bubbly. Feeling the moment, I grab a glass from the tray.

Aaries grabs the glass from me before it gets to my mouth.

M grabs the glass from him. "Nice try. Both of you. Unless it's water, you're not drinking it." M sniffs it, shrugs, and downs it. "Anything I need to know about?"

"Just some conversation. With Fury and Jared."

"Oh." A glint catches in M's eye.

"They said they're in some mentoring program with Clarence Walls." I snatch several shrimp from a passing server and hold up a finger for her to wait while I shuck the empty tails back onto her tray for disposal. The server shoots darts at me as her eyes go from me to the tails back to me. I wave my thanks. "There he goes now with his pastor buddy."

"Two peas," M says.

"I just realized that something don't make sense." I mumble as I chew.

"What's that?"

"At the neighborhood meeting Mr. Walls said there wasn't enough parking for Clifton Corner. But I pass by there several times a day and there ain't any business."

"And yet I hear Mattea's bringing him on as a consultant on the park situation." M strokes his beard.

"To consult on what?" I ask.

"No one knows what consultants do. They just get checks to do it."

Everyone takes their seats. The servers deliver more food. After a few minutes, Mattea climbs up on the dais. Her talk is boring, until she says something about one point five million dollars, and I try to pay more attention. She introduces the governance board members—the folks who control the money. When Ms. Campbell's name falls out her mouth, I notice Ms. Campbell's sitting next to Mattea and Rev. Taft, also on the committee.

Lost in Mattea's droning, I can't help but keep thinking about that money. Over a *million* dollars in a fund. What if whatever's going on is bigger than I thought? I mean, we're not talking about donating uniforms to a youth program in order to get a permit approved or something. There's big money at stake. The rise of applause snaps me out of my thoughts. Mattea locks on to M as she descends from the podium and makes a beeline for him. I step between them and she stops short.

"This has to be terribly boring for you," Mattea says.

"It has its moments. Is that shrimp wrapped in bacon?" I scoop one from her plate. I wave down one of the servers to see if I can find some more.

Staring at her plate like I just spit on it, Mattea sets it down with a pile of uneaten food still on it. The servers come to clear it away. I could eat for days on what folks are just leaving around. This party, all this food, means nothing to them.

"Hi, Bella. Glad to see you here tonight. I wasn't expecting that." Ms. Campbell walks up to join us.

"Everything's a surprise to everyone these days. I just figured out the neighborhood association's been hiding money from folks," I say.

Ms. Campbell turns to M, bewildered.

"You'll have to excuse our friend here. She's a little amped up," he says.

"You have that effect on people," Mattea chimes in.

"She's still figuring out the scale of how TIFs work," M says.

"Nobody is hiding anything. After all, we got that annual Northwest Planners board meeting coming up," Ms. Campbell announces, a little too loudly. She

133

gives me a long knowing look, like she's trying to send me a message that I don't understand. "Everything is public record. If you want a copy of anyone's proposal, come by the library office and pick it up tomorrow. Anybody can request that. Ain't that right, Mattea?"

Mattea shoots her a hard glance before recovering. "Yes."

Ms. Campbell rests a hand on my shoulder. "You still trying to get money for an art program? What's the obstacle?"

"People like her." I point at Mattea.

"Girl, you love the drama of a scene. Just like your momma." Mattea tips another glass to her lips, unflustered. "We all used to come round the Ryder place back in the day."

The nerve of her letting my mom come across her lips. The way she says the words feel like a threat she's hinting at. Acting like she knew her or something. I'm so mad, I can barely see straight. The back of my throat clenches. Sometimes life leaves you no other choice and you have to tell an adult about themselves.

"You and your crew out here lining up to rob the neighborhood to make your own pockets fat," I start in. Loudly. "Carving up the neighborhood, dealing out crumbs while sweeping us under the rug. But you just a crook. Doing to us what everyone before you did. Got all your people eating except the community."

Needing something to throw, I reach for a tray of leftover food. M wraps an arm around my waist to usher me out of Mattea's range before the shock of my outburst sinks in. Especially in front of so many of the shot callers she was trying to impress. She might lose the rest of her mind, whip off her wig, and go all in on me despite how young I am.

Tipping his hat to Ms. Campbell, M says, "I think it's time for us to go."

I JERK MYSELF FREE from M and storm to the curb. All I can do is pace impatiently. My eyes burn a hole into the valet as Aaries hands him the tag to bring the truck around. Once it arrives, the valet holds the door for M while I stomp around to my side. Yanking on the door handle and, finding it locked, I kick the tire. I'm about to kick it again when Aaries remote-unlocks the doors. I tumble into the back seat, cross my arms, and stare out the window.

"What did you gain from that?" M hands me a plate of snacks he must have snatched from a server on his way out. I leave him suspending the plate.

"It felt good." I watch the passing traffic. Without thinking about it, I grab a few shrimp from the plate.

"How did that serve what you're trying to do?" M asks in that calm, unflustered way of his. His voice bubbles with a joke he refuses to share.

I kick Aaries's seat. "If you're just going to lecture me all the way home, you can just drop me off here."

"What lecture? I've asked two questions." Covering his face with his red fedora, M settles into his seat like he's about to take a nap. His voice a little muffled by the hat. "We in your playbook, not mine."

"So, you think I screwed up." I lift my backpack from the floor to my lap. He can play it cool all he wants, but I know when my mouth gets me into trouble and I've let people down.

"We all screw up. I'm not sweating that. Now make no mistake, you definitely left . . . an impression. What I'm trying to get at is what did you learn?"

I hate most of what just happened. I have all these worries and doubts and anger, and if I open my mouth, they'll all come spilling out. The only thing I trust myself to say is, "It's all so big."

"What do you mean?"

"You get all these people running around looking out for themselves. Period. They say they're about community, but . . . nah. I don't trust that business

137

dude Walls or the pastor. And Mattea's the ringleader, directing folks here and there. She's like a person in church who slides out a little for herself every time the collection plate passes by. All the politics and money . . . that's up there." I wave my hands above my head. "Where I'm at down here, I'm just worried about where I'm going to lay my head or get my next meal. Survival stuff. But they out here playing games with people's lives. It's so big and it makes me so . . ." I kick Aaries's seat.

"What is it you are trying to do about it?" The way M slouches, his hands conducting again, it's like he's listening to his favorite song, but the only words he knows well enough to sing out loud are questions.

"Something important."

"What does that mean?"

"I don't know." I throw my hands up, then drop them into my lap with a lengthy sigh. I don't know where I belong. I need to figure out what I'm supposed to do. "Thing is, I need to do more than just survive. We all do. We need things like art and . . . community. I want to improve my neighborhood and I want us to do it together."

"And you're what? Thirteen?" M leans back.

He makes an odd smirk. I can't tell if he's amused, annoyed, or approving. "A lot of pressure you're putting on yourself. What's your plan? Besides you quit kicking the brotha's seat."

I stop myself from another spiteful kick and make a noise somewhere between a grunt and sigh. "I don't know. Is that all right?"

"It's honest. Take your time. Assess what you know. You'll come up with something. Like I said, we're going in your flow."

M always comes at me indirect. That's not the way I'm used to adults dealing with me. He never seems to want anything and leaves things for me to take the lead on. There's a heaviness to it, like a weighted blanket.

When we get back to the neighborhood, I make Aaries drop me off on the corner and wait until they're out of sight before I creep into the Ryder house. The air's humid and slightly musty. I light a candle and sit at the table in the center of the dining room. A thin layer of dust covers everything. I feel it on my hands. I thumb through a few of the photos and sketches scattered along the table. Setting my journal on my right and my cell phone (down to a 17 percent charge) in my lap, I play and replay the park footage. I take notes by candlelight. And think. With my jazz council for company, I recap my observations about everything so far.

"I don't know what M expects from me. I'm still trying to figure this all out and my place in all this mess."

Grover's head angles to the side, its weight not quite supported by his body. Streaks of green dot his face like bleaching tears.

"That neighborhood meeting was a mess. I don't see how anything ever gets done."

Originally, I just wanted to pull together my neighbors to create a mural or something. Create a piece that reminds people that we're here, that our lives matter. Then Mattea decided to get in the way. So I made bringing her down my personal mission. But the more I learn, the more pieces I realize are in play, the larger the puzzle gets. Now things seem to sprawl all over the place and I need to make sense of it all. I keep thinking I've missed something.

I start to make a list of all the players. Lists always help me make sense of things. Jotting down names and any information I know about them, I feel like I'm in school again. The way it wastes so much with us waiting around or doing busy work, it's like it's training us for a life of meetings. "These people have meetings to schedule when they want to have other meetings."

I get up to clear my head a bit and to adjust a few of Grover's rivets that look like they're about to fall off his chest. Returning to the table, I make columns for Mattea and Walls, adding my guesses about what they want. Though I end up writing "money" under both.

"Then there's that park. The place is a wreck. Like someone's putting on a play about parks and only built the bare minimum scenery."

I add Ms. Campbell, the pastor, and even Pass. Slowly a pattern starts to take shape within the lists and names. Now it becomes a kind of same, almost like a puzzle. I jot down Blake Harrison, since M mentioned him and CISC, just to make sure I remember his name. Details are important to keep straight.

"Mattea's a straight-up tax. I can't stand her. She lives by the park. Sorta. She has a house there, but it don't seem at all lived in. And she's connected. Got the police taking orders from her. Clarence Walls sucking up to her."

I add the word *power* by her name. And *control*. It's like the way the Queens operate at school. All the gossip, all the deciding what's cool, even which boys were worth talking to—they all run through them.

Then there's Walls.

"He makes my skin crawl, too. And he got that pastor on payroll."

I flick the padlock in Sarah's chain-link hair. Her fence-post legs are crossed, one over the other. Her shoe dangles from her foot. She's relaxed and in her thoughts.

"But I have folks on my side."

I draw one of those circle diagrams. With Ms. Campbell on one side, I put M in the middle. Making another circle I overlap his with Aaries.

"Aaries is cool. Protective, like a big brother. Smart, too, but he don't like to let on. Keeps real quiet an' all. It's in his eyes, though. They always watching, not missing a thing. And if he ain't looking at you, it's 'cause he's concentrating on listening to you."

Wes's bucket head seems more dented than usual. It may be the flicker of the candlelight, but the way he hovers over me, he reminds me of a teacher checking over my work.

"Of course, he picks all that up from M. It's like he been trained by the old man his whole life. No, I'm not jealous. That ain't the right word. Besides, I'm right there in whatever class they got going on."

I tap my pen against the table. Turning the journal around, I try to study it from different angles.

"I'm starting to like it, I guess."

Hanging out with M and Aaries is the best classroom I've ever had in my life. They make me feel included. Almost like a . . .

"Anyone else?" I announce, jumping out of my seat before I tumble into a dark hole of things I don't want to think about.

I connect a line between folks if they have something in common. Any excuse to draw. Once everything is laid out, the streaks become arrows. All pointing to Mattea. Ms. Campbell remains an unconnected circle, out of the loop. I flip through my notes to remember something she said at the party and realize she told me my next move. Smiling, I head upstairs to slide into my bedroll and set an alarm for early the next morning, hoping my phone charge will hold until then.

My knuckles ache from banging on the metal frame of M's storm door. I'm not even sure I'm making enough noise to let anyone know I'm out here. Listening carefully, I can almost make out Thmei's muffled whines. I wind up to start police-pounding when a bleary-eyed Aaries stumbles out of Ms. Campbell's house. Wearing a dingy tank top and jeans, he rubs his eye and wipes his hand on his shirt.

"You look amped." He yawns.

"And you look like a Milk Dud. M up?"

"Always." Unlocking the door, Aaries holds it open for me. "He has a strict routine. He's probably on his third cup of coffee by now."

He shuffles back toward the hallway. Thmei barks

and scratches from behind a closed door. Aaries tells her to settle down. Instead, she attempts to slide as much of her face under the door as possible. Leaving him to his morning Thmei routine, I head into M's office.

Not bothering to budge from his monitors, M talks as soon as I enter the room. His calendar fills an entire screen. The 8 a.m. hour is blank. "We have an appointment today?"

"Yes. Down at the Public Library No. 1 Center," I say.

"Do we now?" M revolves in his chair, intrigued. His eyes are full and bloodshot, as if he can't pick the idea of sleep out of a lineup. "Is this a formal meeting?"

"Nah. Casual. We need to get a copy of the committee minutes since, like Ms. Campbell said, they're public information. And do it before someone thinks of calling ahead to warn anyone to shred them or something."

Once he stands, M's pants sag. They don't quite fit right, and his shirt desperately needs ironing. Aaries pops back in to inspect him, rebuttoning M's shirt. M slips on his red hat. "Then I'm dressed. Let's go."

I'd grown a little nervous when, at M's suggestion, we drove by Mattea's house. But I didn't see her car. Mattea rarely makes an appearance before 10 a.m., M had commented. Those "Ms. Odom" plates aren't at the center when we arrive either.

The receptionist promptly opens the doors at 8 a.m. "Who might you be?" the round-faced woman with smooth brown skin and an infectious smile greets us as she heads back to her desk. She's the kind of person that lights up when a person walks in.

"My name is Bella Fades." I mirror her smile. I have my tricks, too. Doing what people do, even when they don't realize you're doing it, puts them at ease. "This is my granddad."

Leaving Aaries in the car, M totters a few steps closer. He grasps for a handrail of some sort. I take his hand and steady him at the desk. He tips his hat to her. We've fallen into a perfect routine. A positively adorable picture, if I do say so myself.

"I wanted to get a copy of the last SPIFF. . . ." I turn to him, my innocent face turned up to at least nine. "What was it called?"

"Governance board," M says. "Of the TIF."

"Yeah, the TIF governance board minutes."

"What's a young person like yourself want with boring transcripts? You miss school that much?" The receptionist taps at her keyboard, caught up in whatever's on her screen.

"It's like a summer government class." I dial my cute-girl charm up to eleven. "I was told the meeting was open to the public."

"Yes, I just don't think it's right for a child like you. No offense." The woman glances over at M.

"I'm not the one who's likely to get offended." M redirects her back to me.

I'm starting to lose my patience. Not that I had a lot of calm and cool to begin with, but I feel them about to fray around the edges. I'm beginning to suspect that she's under orders from Mattea to discourage anyone with questions. "I was told to ask for this by Ms. Larrimore."

"What for?"

"For the community." My voice almost raises to turn it into a question as I trip up a little, not sure what kind of answer to give. Then M squeezes my hand. "At that thing last night for your friend,

147

Grandpa. What was his name again?"

"Blake Harrison." M picks up his cue.

"Oh." The woman looks like she swallowed half a lemon by mistake. Pushing away from her desk, she leaves through the door behind her. We hear her rummaging through some files before she brings back a printed copy of the meeting minutes. "Here you go."

The phone on the desk rings. I nearly jump like I saw a snake crawl out of the book stack. "Come on, Grandpa. Let's let her get back to work."

～

I have no idea what I'm reading. This is like when my science teacher passes out a stack of articles and expects me to use them as research. Meanwhile I'm just staring at the pages, feeling like I need a translator. The first thing I do is take pictures of the pages while charging my phone. Once that's done, I spread the papers in front of me so I can take them all in.

It doesn't help. I offer to read a few bits to M, but all he wants to hear are the boring parts.

"Ms. Campbell. Mattea. Clarence Walls." I read off who was in attendance. "I'm not sure I understand any of this. Walker Lofts. Riverside Market.

This subcommittee is a group within the board that decides what the whole even sees. It's a confusing way to organize. It leaves three people in charge and lets two people block everything." I sigh. "All the votes keep going two to one. That's got to be Ms. Campbell against. Everyone else seems to be carving out their slice of the neighborhood pie. Between Mattea and Clarence and something about a school."

"What sort of school?" M perks up.

"I don't know. I mean, we already have Persons Crossings, not to mention a half dozen other schools around here."

"All of which are already underfunded."

"Yeah, there's already not enough . . ." I stop as everything clicks into place.

"What is it?" M asks.

"The money. They want to use the money to open their own charter school."

"Another school doesn't sound bad." M smirks, already knowing the answer. He's testing me. "A charter school can be owned by a small group, but it still has to serve the public."

"My school could use the money. For new books, computers, teachers."

"So, what does that tell you?"

"That I'm about sick of hearing questions like that?"

M shakes his head. "What else?"

Part of me wants to show them some benefit of the doubt. Like they might be doing the right thing for the right reasons and I just can't see the big picture. But right now, they looking all kinds of shady.

"It keeps coming back to the money. It's like they've been put in charge of a bunch of piggy banks that they take turns robbing." I fumble around, looking for something to use to illustrate my point. I decide just to fold pieces of paper in half as a tent. "They supposedly spent one piggy bank on the Hinton park. But since they probably used it to give out favors to each other, maybe broke a piece off for Walls, they got nothing to show for it." I line up two more tents. "They lean on the state's piggy bank to finish the park before anyone notices they ain't did nothing. Because they want to save their main piggy bank for this school project. One point five million of lining their own pockets or building something to stick their name on."

"So? That's the game."

"The game leaves nothing here for the rest of us. They plan to make it sound like it's a new proposal, but they got it all mapped out. No money for any other neighborhood programs. And . . ." I flip back through the proposal. The location of the proposed school is in the middle of our neighborhood. "They'd tear down the Ryder house, Write On the Poetry Spot, and some homes on the block to build their new school. *We all used to come round the Ryder place back in the day.* "These people need to be exposed. Especially Mattea. I can't stand her."

"But you have to be careful how you do it. I know how prone you are to kicking things." Glancing over to Aaries, M raises a lone finger. "But you keep kicking a hornet's nest, you might get stung."

～

The sun beats down on me as I walk back to the Ryder house. There isn't a lot of shade cover from any of the trees along the way. It only makes me simmer all the more, like a pot left on its own on a stove. All I wanted to do was be more a part of the community. Do something that let me feel connected to my mom. Her legacy. I'd done things Ms. Campbell's way—went to meetings, presented my case—and all I got was shut down. They made me feel like I didn't have a voice. The people with money could build useless parks or centers. They could support themselves but not the neighborhood. Not the kids on the block. Not me. And I won't be powerless.

I slide into my study nook and read and reread the documents on my phone. My blood threatens to boil and bubble right out of my veins, and an idea strikes me. There's more than one project that could pull the community together. I don't have a fancy computer setup like M, but I can't use his anyway.

Not for what I have in mind.

"WHO NEEDS CLOTHES?" a volunteer at Outreach asks. It's the next day, I have clothes to wash, and I don't recognize this lady. There's a lot of turnover among the staff, let alone the volunteers. Probably six to nine months before they burn out. Turns out dealing with teens who live on the streets takes a high "emotional toll" on folks.

Imagine being one of the teens.

Word is that the folks at Outreach don't ask too many questions, and I knew that I could suffer through a few prayers and verses to grab a meal, take a shower, and maybe get my laundry done. There's an entire network of churches and organizations I loop through, so I know the deal. They say they don't report to DCS, but I have to be careful. I keep it simple, assure them that I'm fine. And safe. Eat, do laundry, add some minutes to my phone, grab some fruit and water to go.

I erase my name from the "Washer" column on the posted sign and scratch it under the "Dryer" as I transfer my clothes. Next to the sign hangs a painting that reads, "Believe there is good in the world."

The smells of eggs, sausage gravy, and biscuits draw me to the kitchen. I have never smelled anything better. Not just 'cause I'm hungry—even school cafeteria food smells good when I'm hungry—but the way the volunteers here fuss over getting it right and serving us almost feels like home. I grab a plate and settle on a couch by their chapel. I can see the mural in the lobby from here—the word *hope* so stylized it takes a while to see the letters in the swirls of violets and magentas. I recognize the artist's handiwork. Dude by the name of Chad. I've seen his tags around. I start to size up the blank wall in front of me, imagining what I'd paint.

A scruffy dude in a Reggie Miller jersey jumps up, shouting at the boy at the table next to him. "I told you to quit staring at my girl."

The dude's a regular around here, but I wouldn't even call him an associate, since he stays steady beefing. When I see him out and about, I make it a point to get ghost.

The pregnant girl next to him keeps her head down and shovels eggs into her mouth. She's not claiming either one of them. She follows my personal philosophy: the best way to stay out of fights is to avoid them.

"If you ain't man enough to keep her, ain't no point in being mad at me." It takes me a minute to realize that it's Jared. My heart sinks in my chest, a mix of surprise and fear making it pound so hard it hurts. Not 'cause I'm afraid of him. That fool wouldn't make my upper lip twitch in his direction. But the idea of him seeing me here makes me feel exposed. Like he'd have something over me. A secret to hurt me with.

I slump into my seat, making myself small and praying that he doesn't recognize me. I know he's not homeless. Knowing his selfish butt, I bet he probably heard about a free meal and coasted through.

"Sit down before you get folded. You don't want this smoke."

Staff members are already rushing to step between them. But Scruffy Dude's been called out. He steps up to Jared. They get to within an inch of each other, no hands thrown. Though they're the same age, Scruffy Dude has a couple inches on Jared. I can't tell if one loses his balance while trying to puff up big or just doesn't realize how close they actual are when they try to flex, but they manage to bump.

Then fists fly.

They punch at each other in sloppy windmilling motions. Laughing the whole time, Jared works at yanking the Reggie Miller jersey over the dude's head. It's always the small ones that scrap the hardest, because they have something to prove. Him even more since he has a rep on the streets he's trying to build up. Everywhere he goes, he wants his name to ring out as a threat. I'm trying to get a good look while keeping low at the same time. The two spill outside with kids following them to cheer the fight on, but the counselors separate them once they're outside. Still grinning, Jared flips his hood over his head and bounces. Everyone huddles about outside.

"Bella! I didn't think I'd see you 'round these

parts." I jump at the familiar voice. Ms. Campbell's standing over me.

I can feel the walls between my worlds starting to crumble. Like it's only a matter of time before everything falls apart. Uncurling in the seat, I straighten so that I look more like a cat stretching after a nap and lie fast.

"I came in to see about doing an art piece. I figure if they let Chad tag a wall, they might want someone who actually knows how to paint." Struggling to keep from studying her face to see if she's buying it, I wave her to the empty seat across from me. "What are you doing here?"

Hovering while still giving me room, Ms. Campbell doesn't make a thing of it. "I'm new. They brought me in part-time as the women's intake coordinator."

"That right?"

"I'd love to talk more. Maybe figure out a way to do your art project here."

"I can't stay. I'm just waiting for . . ." I pause, careful not to admit that I know Jared. I shift to keep my plate hidden behind me. "All them to clear out farther down the block before I head out."

I avoid her eyes. It's one thing to know my situation, another to be defined by that. I want her to see Bella. Not homeless Bella. Not broken Bella.

"Mm-hmm." She has that Big-Momma-about-to-bust-all-my-lies grumble building.

"I need witnesses!" Officer Squirrel 'Stache bursts into the lobby, yelling. "There was a fight that went down here and we need to sort who's going downtown. Or you all are."

Ms. Campbell jumps up to rush over to him. "No, we aren't doing things like that. Not in here."

While her back is turned, I run to the dryer to toss my clothes into my bags. Slipping a couple bottles of water and some fruit into my backpack for later, I slide out the side door.

My next stop is the downtown library. It's always been a safe haven. When it's open, I can use its bathrooms or its computers and I'm completely invisible. I don't want anything to track back to M. My plan is to build a generic website from a template on one of those free sites so that I can post the documents online. Maybe that way I can start to get the word out. Anonymously, since no one would take a kid seriously.

After creating a fake account, I post links to it in a few Facebook groups and in the Nextdoor for the Northwest Planners and King's Crossing neighborhoods. Where old people would see it. But I don't know what else I can do to make sure the word gets out.

Using a pass I got from Outreach, I hop onto

the IndyGo bus, and before long, I realize that I'm humming one of the songs from the frog choker's album. After dropping off my laundry at the Ryder house, I check up and down the block. No one's out, but I can't help but feel as if I'm being watched. My instinct tells me to stay in very public spaces.

Before I finish walking up M's porch steps, Aaries opens the door, bows, and sweeps his hand out like he's a butler.

"Milady," he says.

"Can't you ever be normal?" Distracted by my own smart mouth, I stumble on the first step and whack my knee, dropping my backpack.

Aaries reaches for it, and I have a moment of panic. It's as much of everything I call home stuffed into one place as I can. In case I need to run off on no notice. He stops, hand still out, but hovering above it. "I can carry your bag every now and then. But only if it's okay with you."

"It's . . . okay."

He lifts it onto his back. "Let me know when you want it back. Or if it just starts to bother you. I know I'd feel some sort of way trusting someone with my stuff."

Especially all of my important things, I almost say, but his slight nod tells me he already knows. I play-punch him in the side.

"What's that for?" he asks.

"Just making sure I'm not dreaming."

"But you hit *me*?"

"I'm making sure you awake, too."

"That makes no . . ." Shaking his head, he turns his hand out for me to lead the way. "Fine. After you."

I wonder if this is what it's like to have a brother.

Thmei brings me a ratty, chewed-up piece of rope and drops it at my feet. It makes a wet sound when it hits the floor. She's been slobbering into it for a while. Staring at it, then me, and back to it, she crouches beside the rope. Waiting. She yips, a high squeaking bark she cuts short so it's not too loud. I make a pincer out of my thumb and index finger because I know I'll regret grabbing that sloppy mess, but as soon as I reach for it, she grabs it and runs to the couch. I think she's playing keep-away with me.

"This makes two mornings in a row you here," M yells out from his office. "Well, just after noon, anyways. It's not like we punch a time clock around here. Anything wrong?"

"Nah. Just wanted to work over here. Figure some things out."

Aaries shares a look with M and sets my bag onto the couch. Once he scoots out of the way, I fall down next to it. Thmei inches closer to me, nudging the toy toward me.

"Uh-huh." M has that *I already know* tone, always suspecting something, but he lets it go. "You come up with a plan?"

"The beginnings of one. Maybe. I wanted to try something on my own first." My phone is at 81 percent after charging it at Outreach. I scroll through Instagram to check in on my associates from school. It's all pictures of summer camps, get-togethers, and trips to amusement parks. None with room for me. A couple had DMed me about hanging out, but it's not like I could invite any of them over. Even the idea of visiting *their* houses fills me with a rising terror that makes it hard to catch my breath. It's like I'm convinced that just being around them, they'll just *know* I'm homeless. Visible to everyone like sweaty pit stains.

"We got company." M's words intrude on my thoughts. He points to his screen. "Your friend is on her way up."

That didn't take long. It's Mattea, banging on the storm door. The way she lays into it, it's the door feeling it, not her knuckles. Thmei leaps off the couch. I can't tell if she's scrambling for the front door or to duck under M's bed as Aaries moves to answer Mattea's knocking. She steps back and glares straight into one of the cameras, her face filling one of M's monitors. "Ain't no point in not answering. I know you're in there."

People were bound to be upset. I didn't know who might come knocking, but I figured the one hurt most might. Their meeting notes make them look bad. Like they won't let any money flow into the community. I try to hide my pleased grin.

Heavy footfalls stomp across the wood floors. By the time I see them again, Aaries is holding Thmei back by her collar. He glances between Mattea and the dog, as if wondering who is in more danger of being bit. He drags Thmei to a back room and shuts her in, allowing Mattea to barge into M's office.

"What you on, M?" she yells.

"Why does the Voice of the People have to be so loud?" Bored and tired at the same time, M turns around, his already-over-her face firmly in place.

"To make sure that I'm heard. No one's going to get one over on me. Not today. Not tomorrow. Not ever." She makes a point of not looking at me.

"What are you going on about, Mattea?"

"You see this?" She waves her phone about. "Because there are younger ears in the room, I won't say what I want to say. But M, seriously, this kind of stunt, what are you trying to gain?"

"Still don't know what you on about."

"That the way you want to play it? What, you think I wouldn't find out?" Mattea began to pace in front of the couch. I tuck my legs under me so she doesn't brush against them.

"If I admit I did it, would that make this conversation stop?" Leaning forward, M rests his chin on his clasped hands.

"I already know you did it. You all but signed your name to it. Like it was a huge coincidence that a little girl and her 'grandpa'"—Mattea spits those last syllables—"come in for the minutes of our governance meeting one day and the next day they end up posted on the internet."

M absorbs the information without betraying even a glimpse at me. But it's almost as if I can feel

164

the full weight of his consciousness shift toward me. "Well, now we're clear on what we're dealing with."

"We sure are. I need you to take it down."

"Why? It's public information," I ask, stalling to give M time to consider his options. I shift on the couch, suddenly unable to get comfortable.

"Consider it my favor." Mattea levels her eyes at him.

They stare at each other. The silence stretches into something that makes me uneasy.

"I see." Even without glancing at me, I know he's waiting for my permission. With Mattea's attention focused on him, she doesn't see me nod. He stretches like he's trying to work a kink out of his back. "I'll see what I can do. Reach out to some folks. Have it down before the day's over."

"How about within the hour?" Mattea presses. "You have no idea the folks this mess upset."

"Yeah, I do. Your Massa got upset and yanked a leash. Set all of his dogs loose." M grins but his smile has no chill to it.

"M, child or no child, I will cuss you straight into next week if you don't watch yourself." Mattea folds her arms and waits.

M raises his hands in mock surrender. "It'll be down in an hour."

"I have your word?" Mattea arches a still-skeptical eyebrow.

M lifts his chin. "Word is bond."

Mattea cuts her eyes at M and then sideways at me. She turns on her heel and brushes past Aaries, shouting, "And make sure that girl comes by soon to repaint my house."

M studies the doorframe as if she might charge back in like an angry girlfriend who remembered one more point in her argument. But the footage of Mattea stomping down the porch steps to climb into her car plays out on one of his monitors. A minute after the door shuts, M sighs and returns to his work. He doesn't spare a glance my way nor make any comment. Even without him yelling or anything, I feel like I'm not off the hook. The silence twists up my insides.

"M, I'm sorry." My voice snags over each of the words.

"For what?" M keeps his back to me. "You tried to pull a gangsta move and almost pulled it off. In fact, you got me out of her favor debt nice and easy.

Still, you just need to think through some of the possible consequences a bit more."

That overwhelmed, out-of-my-depth feeling hits me again. There's a chorus in my head that gets too loud. The way Mattea's antics got under my skin. Walking in here like she's better than us. Better than me. It makes me so heated, I want to scream. "Why don't you just say it?"

"Say what?" M turns to me, confused.

"That I'm not smart enough to take her down on my own."

He holds his hands out. "Bella, I—"

"You already decided what you think, so I'm going to go for a walk." I need to clear my head. At school I have an accommodation that allows me to leave my seat and go into the hallway whenever I need to "reset" (which is school code for cooling off before I explode on someone). I'm definitely in need of a reset. Or three. "Here's the log-in info for the site. I'll be back. Maybe then you'll want to hear what I got to say. Or we don't have to talk about it."

SO MANY FAMILIES used to live here in The Land, generation after generation, way my mom used to tell me. Now the neighborhood is full of ghosts, and not just the ones I'm pretty certain hang out around Crown Hill Cemetery (which is why I never cut through that area at night). Abandoned houses are the ghosts of families who used to live around here. The boarded-up businesses are the ghosts of folks who wanted to be their own boss and build something they could call their own. Ghosts stalk the streets as cracked sidewalks, broken streetlamps, bus stops fallen into disrepair, overgrown embankments, and all the other signs that we've been forgotten. It's easy to feel like one of them: alone and abandoned. A ghost in my own neighborhood.

On my good days, I know—deep in my heart—that I'm smart. But I also know when I'm struggling. I've been watching M. Studying the way he does things. But whenever he's not around, when I try the things I think I've learned, everything falls apart, and I can't wrap my hands around what's not working. That's how a bad day starts. With that little voice in my head that says it's my fault. That there's something wrong with me.

I keep walking the neighborhood, not knowing exactly what I'm searching for, only that I need a distraction. But it's summer, and the days are long, hot, and boring. I can't quite say I miss school—with all its rules and people telling me what to do and when—but I miss having my days be steady. Knowing what to expect.

My steps take me back over into Golden Hill to Bertha Ross Park, following the sounds of little kids screaming and yelling at each other while they play. An older man perches on a bench like an eagle guarding a nest. Ms. Campbell once told me that he used to be her third-grade teacher before he retired. After about twenty minutes, he gathers all the kids. He opens a book and starts reading to them. They swarm, elbowing each other to sit closer. It's a book I read in class last year, pretty advanced for them. But he pauses as he reads. Asks them to tell him back what he read, explain it scene by scene. Has them guess at what some of the hard words mean. They're in school but don't know it, so they enjoy it. Kind of like I am with M. I fish in my backpack for my sketch pad and a charcoal stick. I draw the scene. After twenty minutes, he sends them off to play again.

The wind shifts toward me, carrying the dirt smell of vegetables mixed with the floral scent of peonies. I wander down the street where the gardeners live. The couple's out in their yard, never far from one another. I can't help but watch them, and begin sketching them, too.

"What are we going to do next? Are you almost finished?" the woman fusses at the old man. She has a slight hunch to her shoulders, like the effort to fully straighten isn't worth it. Her thin wrinkles around her mouth and eyes remind me of spiderwebs. Her broad straw hat shades her face but highlights the ruby lipstick she wears.

"I just need the water." His voice is relaxed; he's long used to being bossed around by her.

"I see that." She hands him the hose.

"Where's the row over here? I don't want to drown them and knock the seeds out."

"Right in front of you." The words sound scolding, but the playfulness in her voice takes out any sting. They are so caught up in the rhythm of their back and forth that it takes a while for her to notice me. "We have a visitor."

"Who?" is all he manages to squeeze out as he works to get to his feet. The struggle is real. He's almost out of breath, but he makes it. He easily stands a foot taller than his wife. He's bald with a thick white mustache, neatly trimmed. His amber complexion complements her auburn one. They have an easy blend of colors that set each other off.

"Hi, my name is Bella," I say nervously, remembering M's encouragement about never being afraid to sign my work. Let them know who I am. "I've seen you around but we've never really met."

"Ben and Georgia Taylor." He wipes a thick sheen

of sweat away with his gloved hand but takes off the glove to shake mine.

It feels weird even to think of calling adults by their first names. Especially when I hang out with teachers, it's always Mr. This or Mrs. That. Maybe I've gotten more used to it spending so much time with M. But I like it. It makes me feel on their level. "I've always loved your gardens. How long have you been doing it?"

"I was born and raised on a farm," Georgia says. "But my father and brothers did all that work. I wasn't trying to be out in the heat picking green beans and stuff. Now look at me."

"Forty-three years. The entire time we been married," Ben said.

"The entire time we been in this house," she echoes.

I point to the rows that extend into the neighboring lot. "It looks like you've spread out."

"The Washingtons used to live there, but the house is empty now. The rest of us are using their yard as a community garden. We keep the yard looking nice and everyone who grows helps take care of it.

The Latina lady the next house over lets us run hoses from her house to handle watering it."

"We have four other gardens, but this one's just for The Land." Ben gives a nod. "Even got our grandson Fyzle working on a spot."

The boy who had his bike's wheel bearings stolen stumbles out of the back patio door and makes a visor out of his hand. It takes a minute for him to recognize me.

"Got your bike fixed?" I ask.

"It's all good." He nears and lowers his voice. "Thanks."

"No problem. We're all in this together." I hear Ms. Campbell's words tumble out of me. I almost groan in disgust but realize it didn't feel too bad to say. Or hear. "Y'all growing anything I'd like?"

"Onions, peas, greens, cucumbers, tomatoes, garlic." Ben laughs as my face collapses in disgust.

"But we can't just grow in peace. Someone called the state on us, so we had to get the soil tested. Took a month, but they said it was excellent. Like I needed some test to tell me what good earth was." Georgia grabs a small bale of hay and hands it to me. "Here, if we're going to keep talking, we might as well put you to work. Put some straw down."

"Okay." I jump to it without hesitation. Georgia speaks with the authority of all grandmothers. I'm not sure that I know what I'm doing, but I start spreading hay around, imitating Fyzle.

"See if you can lay the straw so it smothers the weeds. Keep them from growing," he says gently.

"Plus, the straw keeps the water from just evaporating out." Georgia peeps over my shoulder.

"Okay." I scatter hay carefully, getting it between rows, not covering any sprouting plants. Georgia lingers for a moment longer but must trust me enough that she turns back to her work. "So, what else do you do?"

"We own— I guess I ought to get used to saying *used to* own . . . ," Ben says.

"We still own it. I ain't giving up," Georgia snaps.

"We own," Ben corrects himself, "the Village Bodega. Over there on Clifton Street and Thirtieth."

"I know it. Over by Clifton Corner," I say.

I'm not sure what the look means that passes between them, but something bitter twists at the corner of Georgia's mouth. I take a chance, hoping they'll open up a bit. "I've met that Clarence Walls. He's . . . a piece of work."

I don't hide how disgusted he makes me, but I feel pretty proud that I didn't spit after saying his name.

"He sure is." Ben relaxes a bit. "Been fussing at us, trying to get us to sell our spot to him. We told him no, because after the Double 8 closed, The Land doesn't have any grocery stores over here. It's important that we have somewhere that still sells food."

"We sell produce from all the gardens," Georgia adds. "Lift everyone up."

This is where they want to put the parking lot. Taking away our last market.

"Yeah. Walls didn't take 'no' none too well. That's when them boys started bothering us. And then all of a sudden, the zoning changed, just like it did over there at that corner with the old poetry place. And now they tell us that we have to close down."

"Wait, what boys?" I perk up to full attention, though based on the way my stomach feels like a big rock just dropped into it, I already know who they mean.

"The ones on the bikes," Georgia says.

"Say the devil's name and he shows up." Ben nods

toward the end of the block. "Or, rather, *they* do."

Jared and Fury circle once at the beginning of the block. I'm guessing that they're making sure that the streets are clear before they pedal toward us.

"I'll talk to them. You all go inside." Scattering the last of my straw in a hurry, I brush my hands off on my shorts.

"Why don't we all go inside?" Ben says. "That way there won't be no trouble."

"It's okay. I got this. I know them."

"You take care, child." Georgia's already at her patio door. "Those two ain't got no home training."

I wait until the Taylors make it inside before I start walking toward Jared and Fury.

I'm about to violate my reset.

20

CLOSING THE GARDEN gate behind me, I slow walk to cut off the boys. "What do you two want?"

"We got no business with you," Fury says, his voice serious as a tornado.

"For now," Jared says.

"I got time." I block the gate.

"We just need to talk to them."

"Why?" I don't have a chance to think up a good strategy. I'm going to have to improvise. I stand tall, making myself as big as possible.

"We sending a message," Jared says.

Fury cuts him a glance like a knife to the throat to shut him up. I don't know why anyone trusts Jared with anything more than a recipe for sugar.

"Why don't you just leave them alone?" I ask. "These are good people."

"Ain't no such thing. Now you need to just mind your own business," Fury's voice was low but intense. Cold.

"Yeah, mind ya business." Jared drifts close enough to shove me. "Just because you a girl don't mean we won't go through you."

There's something mean in Jared's eyes. Dangerous. The kind of look like he's just gotten a whupping and needs to beat someone else to make himself feel better. Like shoving me would only whet his appetite. I tuck my hand into the side pocket of my bag, feeling for my mace, and hold it there as I circle around, both moving away from the Taylors' front door and making sure the wind blows to my back. "Don't do that again."

Jared hops off his bike, letting it fall to the ground. All about business, Fury tries to wave him off, never losing sight of the Taylors' place. Jared stalks a couple steps toward me, each stride full of menace. Like even his walk's supposed to scare me. He cracks his knuckles. "What are you going to do?"

Before he can react, I dart up on him and shove

him hard back into his bike, almost over it. His legs get caught on his pedals, sending both him and his bike into a tangled heap. Fury tries to help him up, but Jared smacks his hands away.

If his eyes were mean before, they're murderous now. The two of them have forgotten all about the Taylors. I just need to survive whatever beatdown they intend. But by the time Jared's on his feet and Fury's able to get back on his bike, I'm in full sprint down the block.

I YANK ON THE plywood covering the front window of the abandoned house just enough to be able to peek out and scan the streets. They'd catch up to me quick if I ran straight to Mr. Ryder's house. Plus, I don't want to blow up that spot. Instead I had cut through the maze of houses, planning to zigzag through the blocks to get back to the side of the neighborhood I know best. Without them realizing it, the boys herded me here. Fury zooms by. Still on foot, Jared checks bushes and porches. They lost track of me but know I have to be close. Checking my phone, I'm down to a 3 percent charge. I punch in Aaries's number.

"Oh, so someone decided—" Aaries's mouth is already off and running.

"I ain't got time to play. It's an emergency." Something just this side of panic fills my hushed voice, which shuts Aaries up. "I need your help."

"What's up?" His voice flips and he's completely serious.

"I'm in a house, corner of Thirty-Third and Clifton. Fury and Jared got me pinned down."

"I'll . . ."

The line goes dead. I hit the power button a few times but nothing lights up. Aaries knows how bad they can get, but I can't just hope that he comes to the rescue. I need to take care of me. I creep back to the window. Jared's thin voice screeches from not too far away. He's still heated and not going to give up soon. Probably the most determined he's ever been to finish a job without pay or threat of a beatdown.

I lean against the doorway as if it might collapse if I don't prop it up, clutching the dead phone to my chest like a set of rosary beads. My heart pounds against my hands and I inhale deeply and let my breath out slowly to try to calm myself. Just in case

Aaries doesn't show, I try thinking of a back-up plan. Closing my eyes, I picture the house, how it's situated on the block, and attempt to imagine possible exit routes. I'd have to slip out the back door to buy myself some extra seconds since I'd be spotted right away if I left out the front. But the overgrown yard would slow me down. If I got across the main street, I might make it to Clifton Corner or get to somewhere else public. They wouldn't dare act too much a fool in Clarence Walls's place. That would mean police and Kevin Paschall sure doesn't want that smoke. My other option is to cut deeper into the neighborhood, where maybe I could make it around to Ms. Campbell's.

The walls of this house are scorched, like they barely survived a fire. The floors aren't much better. I tiptoe across the tattered carpet. Every time I step on a floorboard that creaks, I worry that I might hit a soft spot in the flooring and wind up crashing through to the basement. I peek out the back patio door. Glass no longer fills the windowpane. Plenty of light floods in from the outside. When I lean toward the opening of the window again, a bloodshot eye meets mine.

Jared has found me.

With no time to think, I shove the door open. The action catches Jared off guard. Surprised and off-balance, he yelps as he tumbles into the knee-high grass of the backyard. I dash out, sprinting for the sidewalk. Jared's startled cry causes Fury to screech to a stop, wheel about, and barrel toward me. Scrambling to his feet, Jared tracks me, his steps light in case I try to juke him out of his shoes. A few more steps and he'll be able to grab me.

My survival instinct kicks in. Slipping my phone into my backpack, I retrieve the hidden canister instead. I whip my hand out. Before Jared's brain recognizes the threat it represents, I spray my Mace. I'd been wanting to test it out for a while now anyway. A thin stream arcs from the can. All I can picture is me as Spider-Man shooting my webs into the bad guy's face.

My aim is true.

Jared screams as soon as the spray hits him. Fury leaps from his bike. Without an instant of panic, he races to the nearest hose and drags it over to Jared, who's rolling around in the grass thrashing about. I back up, slowly at first to keep an eye on the scene but speed away as Fury flushes out Jared's eyes and the boy slowly starts to gather himself.

Jared staggers to his feet, lumbering about like some kind of zombie. Fury moves to cut me off from the alley behind the house. Scrambling toward the sidewalk, I think about spraying the rest of my canister of Mace, but I'm scared of the wind blowing it into my face. The yard itself has piles of discarded wood, probably cleared from inside, scattered along the patio. I grab a loose two-by-four.

Keep kicking a hornet's nest, you might get stung.

Fair enough, but I'm about to beat some sense into some not very bright hornets.

Aaries's truck brakes scream with a metallic whine until it stops along the alley beside me.

Without breaking stride, I drop the two-by-four and dive toward the truck bed. My landing squishes the air out of my lungs. But at least there's no wood or other junk back here. Aaries hits the gas as soon as he sees I'm safe.

"Looks like I arrived just in time," he says through the rear window, "to save Jared."

"Yeah. Well, a girl can't just wait around for boys to decide when to be helpful." Counting my heartbeats and struggling to get my breathing under control, I crouch low in the dirty truck bed. The muscles in my body slowly unclench until I'm able to sit upright.

"I see you've been off making friends," M says from the passenger-side seat.

"They don't appreciate my negotiation skills." Facing Aaries, I jab my thumb M's direction. "What's he doing here?"

"He can be pretty spry when he needs to be," Aaries said.

"We were already out running errands when Aaries said he had to make a pickup. I told him that I'd ride along."

Still mad at how close they cut things, especially if they were waiting on the old man, I grumble, "I was trying not to talk to you for the rest of today."

"Well, the Lord works in mysterious ways." M stares out the window. Past Public Library No. 1. Past Clifton Corner. Past Nu Land Missionary Baptist Church. The neighborhood is changing behind the scenes. But folks keep driving along, never slowing down enough to see what's going on. "We here and I can't move time. It's probably not safe in these streets for you."

I slide back low into the truck bed, to think for a minute. "Well, if I'm going to be stuck with you, you have to buy me something to eat."

"No problem," M says. "Off to Burger King we go."

22

I STAND NEAR ENOUGH to M and Aaries for the cashier to know we're one check but still far enough apart from them to let everyone know I'm not in the mood for any of their nonsense. With M buying, I also make a point of ordering the most expensive sandwich on the menu along with a large French fry and a large drink.

"Anything else?" M asks sarcastically.

"An Oreo pie." I bend over the counter and stage-whisper. "Make sure you give him all his change."

M grunts and hands his wallet over to Aaries, who fishes out a credit card.

I grab my cup and wind my way to a table close to an outlet so that I can charge my phone. M slides along the bench to face me. While sucking on a shake, Aaries carries over the tray of food. Without glancing toward him, I slurp noisily through my straw and pass him the empty cup to refill.

"Don't know why you so mad at me," Aaries says. "You the one that got diagnosed with a case of 'ignorant fearlessness.'"

"Boy, boo." I turn to stare at the wall, dismissing him.

Aaries passes a look to M, who shrugs, before leaving to refill my Coke. When he returns, he sets it on the table in front of me and slides into the table behind M. Far enough away where he can pretend to be on his phone, to give us something close to privacy but close enough to still ear hustle. And keep an eye on us and the door. He's a little overprotective.

I hesitate. I know there's a trap in here somewhere. Or one of M's teachable moments that are really starting to get on my nerves.

"What's your deal?" I ask.

"What deal?"

"Going around collecting kids. Get them running your errands. I didn't ask for help."

"I know." M is making an utter mess of his burger. Peeling off the tomatoes and pickles, tearing small bits off at a time.

"What do you get out of it?"

"You."

I just blink at him. "Yeah. I'm gonna need more than that."

"One of the things I've always tried to do was raise up young people. When I was a lawyer, I mentored kids all the time. Even as an investigator, the neighborhood was my classroom. Parents used to bring their kids by like I was an alternative school. Then me and my family had a . . . falling out."

"What happened?" I sit up. I'd been wondering what happened but didn't know how to ask.

"I confronted my brother about what was going on in the community. What he was doing. Boys like Jared and Fury groomed to jump into that life. I got fed up. It got bad."

"You dime him out?"

"I ain't no snitch, if that what you asking." M

189

rears back like he doesn't want even the hint of the accusation to splash on him. "But I was a part of the system until I realized it couldn't get me what I wanted. So I went into . . . private investigation."

"What does that even mean?"

"Do my own digging. Expose what needed exposing. Try to fix what I could fix. That's how things with my brother . . . escalated." M rubbed his bad leg. "Anyway, folks got scared. Afraid to get caught up in . . . family business. But every now and then, someone still falls into my orbit. Like Aaries. Folks that got potential but just need someone to give them a place to get some footing."

"I ain't a charity case." My straw squeaks as I adjust it. A long low whine.

"Never said you were."

"Just wanted to make sure you understand." My straw sucks noisily against the remaining ice.

M tips his hat at me. Closing his eyes, he goes still and silent while I eat. Conducting whatever symphony plays in his head. Almost like he's waiting on something. On me.

"I didn't think it would come back on us.

Especially so quick," I finally say, picking over my remaining fries.

"There's the first lesson." M opens his eyes as if refocusing on the conversation.

"What's that?"

"There's an 'us' now. Your team. You didn't tell us the whole story. That left me—well, more Aaries—on the hook to clean up the mess with the minutes. As a leader, you don't have that luxury. If your team don't know what's up, we don't know how to back your play."

"I ain't no leader neither."

M just lets my words hang there without comment. I'm used to doing things on my own. But M, Ms. Campbell, even Aaries—it's been nice having people fight to be a part of my life. I've been so worried about, I don't know, proving to them that I'm good enough, I haven't paid attention to how hard they're proving themselves to me. I wring my napkin and wipe away the condensation from my cup as well as the pooled rings beneath it. The quiet spreads between us. Not liking how it feels, I interrupt it again.

"What's the second lesson?"

M flicks his gray eyes my direction. "You don't know what you don't know. You don't see how deep the waters are until other people get in and start drowning."

"Then why you got me in the pool in the first place? I'm just a . . ."

M waves me off like he isn't interested in what I'm about to say. "Let me ask you something: how old should you be when you learn to swim?"

"It's not the same." I dip a cold French fry into some ketchup.

"No, it's not. Because here, you always in the water, you just never realized or paid attention. Now you know. You got caught up in its currents and undertows. And yeah, sometimes it's deeper than you're ready for. That's why you make sure there's a lifeguard on duty."

"You know, this is where your comparison starts to break down, right?" A thin smile flashes across my lips.

"Yeah. I couldn't decide between lifeguard and life preserver and lost the thread of it." M softens a little and leans back against his seat.

I get what he's saying. I'm not used to having a team. A . . . I don't know what to call him. "I hate that my idea came back on you like that."

"I was trying to tell you that it was a good plan. Right out of my playbook. The downside is that, well, it's right out of my playbook. I could have warned you that folks would have assumed I did that no matter how careful you were. And, historically, many of my plans have come back to bite me in the butt. Not that I'd ever admit to something like that in public."

"I understand," I say.

"There's an upside." M pauses, allowing his grin to broaden. "Mattea's burned her favor now."

"That's what I don't get. I barely had the pages up overnight. There hasn't been enough time for word to get out. It didn't come close to going viral."

"There's been enough time for *someone* to see it. Basically, the meetings show that they are playing games with the neighborhood's money. They have to answer to folks; that's the way power and politics work. It's not about how many people see it but *who*. Someone with enough clout to rattle Mattea's cage and snap her into action."

"That sounds above me."

"Power works the same at every level. You pushed Jared and Fury. It was only a matter of time before they pushed back. Then things escalate."

Having finished my fries, I begin to nibble from M's tray. I leave him the pile of smaller ones. From the corner of my eye I see Aaries shaking his head but he keeps sucking on his shake.

M's gaze lingers like I'm some math problem he's trying to work out. Feeling the weight of his eyes, I stop chewing to meet his gaze and I wait for the ax to fall for whatever is on his mind.

"You staying in the Ryder house," M says in a low voice. It isn't a question, more a statement awaiting confirmation.

"You going to rescue me?" Raising my straw to my lips, I don't take my eyes from his out of defiance. "I. Don't. Need. Saving."

"Just wondering why there of all the other abandoned houses."

I fidget in my seat. I take another fry and chew on it slowly. "It's kinda like church to me. Mr. Ryder turned everything he found in the neighborhood into art. Things that had been abandoned, he reclaimed and restored into something beautiful. I guess living there is like being transported to somewhere magical."

"How so?"

"It's got all these paintings and drawings and sculptures and photographs. This guy has stuff at the Indianapolis Museum of Art. He was important. But he lived right here in our neighborhood."

"I knew Ryder. That cat was passionate about three things: family, art, and community."

"That's what I'm saying. He had a way of seeing beauty all over the place in all the little details. He always did his thing, no matter what people thought." Embarrassed about how excited I'm getting, I lower my head and reach for another one of his fries.

After considering my words, M wags a fry at me. "This is what I mean about being the neighborhood griot. That why you care so much?"

"My mom taught me to care about this place. I just wanted to do something good for the neighborhood, you know. Something to make my mom proud. Maybe bring her . . ."

M tilts his head slightly, anticipating my next words. His keen attention jolts me from my train of thought. The table reminds me of a desk suddenly, so I channel the spirit of my school principal, Mrs. Fitzgerald. "You all have put me in a— What's the phrase?"

"Compromising position?"

"Yeah."

M smiles at this assessment. "So it's our fault you're caught up in this mess?"

"I'm just saying, ever since I started messing with you two, my whole world has gotten so . . . loud."

"I barely say anything." M holds his hands to his chest in a protest of innocence.

"Yeah, but . . ." I pause. M has a way of making me feel seen in a way that I'm not used to. He doesn't just see my mistakes. He *does* see them, but he doesn't count them against me. I don't feel like a disappointment around him. "You got me so twisted, I'm figuring out my next steps. Trying to think everything through. Get three moves ahead."

"That's a bad thing?"

"No, but . . ." I struggle to find the right word. "You have a way of moving that . . . disrupts. People don't want you in the room. Even at that party. People had smiles on their faces but underneath—and I mean *barely* underneath—they hated seeing you."

"Well, it's hard for us old heads out here. You young folks . . ." M stops mid-joke and his expression gets serious. "People don't give up power easily. They find their spot and grow comfortable. It's rare for folks to think about community first. You know what I first noticed about you was? Your voice. Not everyone can speak to power."

"Well, I learned early on that sometimes you just have to tell an adult to shut up."

M throws his head back in a laugh and claps his hands. "Yeah, but that comes all too easy to some young folks. You know who to say it to and when. People can't just ignore you. That's power."

"I just don't understand why folks keep acting like they do. Sometimes it's not even good for *them*, but they keep on doing stuff that makes things worse."

"Ain't but two keys to know: all life is politics and all life is money. Navigating relationships to get what you want means you need to understand who you're talking to. After that, you need to understand how power flows and to who. Once you get that, you start to pick up how folks are trying to play you."

"Well, I must not know much, because now I got two knuckleheads after me." I recap my encounter with the Taylors and the chase by Fury and Jared.

"I'm afraid it means you know more than you think," M says.

"I'm afraid 'cause they straight-up thugs that'll jump me as soon as they can catch me."

"Not just that. The way you describe the encounter, they were sent. They're just tools."

"Yeah, they are."

"I mean . . ." Thrown off by the comment, M stops short, and his face cracks from a giggle he can't quite stifle. He wags a finger at me. "Anyway, what I'm saying is that Kevin had to have sent them. As a warning."

"Yeah, but . . ." I don't know where I'm going next with my thoughts. I chew on my lower lip while I try to make connections. "Does this mean that Clarence Walls is working with Kevin Paschall?"

"All life is politics . . ."

" . . . and all life is money," I finish. "If I were Kevin, I know I'd want to expand my reach. Get into that legitimate cash game."

"Now you thinking like a real gangsta."

I snatch the longest remaining fry and grind it

between my teeth while I think. "I have video of the James Sidney Hinton Park project."

"Do you now?" M hunches over the table, suddenly curious. "Why?"

"I don't know. Thought someone should document what's been done. Or not done. I feel like nobody sees what's going on there because it's buried so deep in the neighborhood no one can see." I hate that it seems like I don't know what I'm doing. Everything's a frustrating jumble in my head. "If they'd just done what was right by the community, I'd have forgotten I had it."

"Part of navigating politics," M says in a gentle tone that doesn't sound like he's talking down to me, "is the strategic use of the dirt you have on people."

"I want to keep exposing them."

"It's a good start." M makes short work of his fries before I finish them. "But this time we do it in a way only you would do. They won't see that coming."

23

I KNOW FROM THE moment I step into Mr. Ryder's house that something is off. Maybe it's the weird way the light shimmers around the window in the kitchen, like the board no longer covers it right. The way the thin white curtain flutters, catching the glow of the streetlight out back. The glass in a pane has been broken, probably an accident from sloppy entry because they otherwise left everything of Mr. Ryder's alone.

Then I see Wes. He's tipped over, barely held up by the corner he's now slumped into. My heart slams against my chest so hard, I swear my shirt ripples with each beat. Not hearing any movement above me,

I take the stairs two at a time, skipping past Sarah and Grover, and nudge open the door.

My room has been thoroughly tossed. My bags of clothes that I just washed have been scattered. Rifled through, even the pockets turned out. My school stuff has been knocked over, my books flipped over and discarded into a pile. My bedroll, even the rug underneath, has been rooted through. Tears begin to pool in my eyes. My journal with all my notes is missing. All they left was my sketchbook. It was nothing but useless drawings to them.

And then the wave of fear gives way to anger.

Someone hammers on the front door. Firm and loud, but not in the belligerent way that signals the police. I gather myself as best I can and creep down the stairs. I wait a few minutes to see if they will go away.

"Isabella Fades?" a female voice booms. "We know you're in there."

My heart races and I feel like the heat of a spotlight follows me no matter where I go in the room, like there's nowhere to hide. The woman bangs again, more insistent, so I chance opening the door a few inches to peek through.

"Isabella?" The woman steps back into the light from the street as if she doesn't want to startle me. She's about my height, but her business suit can't hide her motherly figure. You know what I mean. Thick arms and a waist that threatens the buttons holding her pants together. Her salt-and-pepper hair, still mostly black, drapes past her shoulders. She tries to soften her stony eyes.

"Who's asking?" I try to sound defiant, but I'm still shaken.

"My name is Lindsey Wong. You can call me Lindsey." She doesn't attempt a smile. She keeps a professional coolness about her, like she's paid to be serious all the time. "I'm with the Department of Child Services."

DCS. I do my best to hide the gulp I can't help but take. I open the door only a fraction more to give my hand room to slip out. "Can I see your identification?"

Lindsey produces her identification without protest. "Here you go."

I have no idea what a real DCS badge looks like, but I go through the motions of a thorough inspection and hand it back. At least her name matches. "Okay, what do you want?"

"We received a report that a minor by the name of Isabella Fades was squatting in an abandoned home."

"Well, I'm not her. Are we done?"

"Even if you're not her . . ." Lindsey allows her voice to trail off as she glances at the officer behind her. My old friend with the squirrel-fur mustache. He nods. "You're still a minor in an abandoned property. At the very least, you're trespassing. You also could be homeless. Why don't you come with us while we sort this out?" She gestures toward her car and I know I don't have a choice.

LINDSEY AT LEAST gives me the chance to grab my backpack before she carts me off. She seems oddly accommodating about it, doing her best to make me feel protected and safe rather than arrested. On the way down to wherever she's taking me, I text M my situation before Lindsey asks me to put my phone away. She assures me that I'm not in trouble or anything like that. Only that a "Child in Need of Services" case has been filed and they are opening an investigation to figure out how best to help me. *We all used to come round the Ryder place back in the day.* Her words take on a new meaning. Mattea.

I cross my arms and stare out the car window until we arrive. The Department of Child Services building looks like a closed-down grocery store that the city has redone as an office, which gets me thinking about the Taylors. Despite all reassurances, the room I wait in reminds me of a police interrogation room, right down to the one-way window, except for the bright colors and toy chest on the opposite side of the room. I plug my phone in. It's up to nearly 90 percent before Lindsey comes back in to check on me.

"I hope you weren't too bored by the wait," she says.

I don't respond, studying the room with only my peripheral vision, trying to keep my eyes down as much as possible. I imagine that a security officer and a social worker are either on the other side of the glass or watching from a nearby room.

"Let's start with your name." Lindsey spreads papers out in front of her, her pen hovering over the first line.

"Joan Watson."

Lindsey sets the pen down on its side. "Joan Watson? I suppose it's a coincidence that that's also the name of a character on the show *Elementary*. I didn't think kids watched that."

"My mother was a fan."

"And what's her name?"

I grow still again.

"Do you mind if I call you Bella?" Lindsey taps her pen against the table while she waits.

I don't respond. Instead I fidget with the bottle of water that's been given to me. The condensation wets my palms and I wipe my hands on my jean shorts.

"We have to figure out who you are. If you don't cooperate, we'll just run your fingerprints."

Look, I'm not here to make her job any easier. Cleaning off the bottle with my sleeved fingers, I stuff my hands into my pockets. I vow not to drink it, so that they can't get my DNA either, since that's how they get criminals on those cop shows.

There's a commotion outside the door. Lindsey excuses herself. A few minutes later, she walks back in followed by M and a sour-faced old white woman wearing orangey makeup that clashes with her box-dyed reddish hair. M sits down beside me while the woman stations herself behind Lindsey. She must be some sort of backup or extra witness. It feels even more like a police interrogation.

"Do you know this man?" Lindsey raises her chin at him.

M gestures that it's okay for me to speak freely.

"Yes, this is M," I say.

"Mr. Menelik Paschall claims to be a lawyer. Hired by a Ms. Essence Campbell on your behalf," Lindsey says.

"Yeah, I keep him on retainer." With M in the room—someone I know is on my side—for the first time I can get comfortable in my chair. Like I can breathe again. I almost smile.

"I doubt that." Lindsey pulls out a pair of glasses from her breast pocket. "What's your relationship with Mr. Paschall?"

"I work with him."

"Doing what?"

"Running errands sometimes, canvassing neighbors. I help him with his computer work because his eyes are bad and he can't edit video for nothing." My head begins to bob, caught up in some jazz melody that floats through my head.

Sensing something has changed, Lindsey softens her voice and takes some of the steel out of her approach. "What's your name, sweetheart?"

"Isabella Fades."

"Glad to officially meet you. Date of birth?"

"June first. I'm thirteen."

"Where were you born?" Lindsey works her way down the form in front of her. It reminds me of when I went through the intake process at Outreach.

"Indianapolis, Indiana."

"Mom and Dad?"

"Eric Turner and Chantal Fades."

"Where are they?"

I glance at Lindsey, over to M, then back to Lindsey. "I kind of don't want to say. I don't want M to find out this way."

"It's okay," he says. "Nothing you tell them will make me think any less of you."

I take a deep breath. "Eric divorced my mom when I was little." My voice hardens. Even my body stiffens. I'm uncomfortable talking about my dad. "He got remarried a couple years later. Stopped coming around as soon as he started his new life. He was killed in a car accident a couple years ago."

"I'm sorry to hear that," Lindsey says.

I try to peek at M, who's as unreadable as Shakespeare. His eyes are glazed over like a smeared chalkboard when the light catches them as he tilts his head my way. His face remains neutral, though. Gentle and without judgment.

"What about your mom?" Lindsey's voice is low, like she doesn't want to scare me off.

"She's . . . not around."

"What does that mean?" Lindsey suspends her pen above the paper, as if to relieve me of the pressure of my words being written down and held against me. Allowing me room to say what I need to say. On my own terms, in my own time. I've tried to forget the last time I saw my mom.

Mom began to withdraw from people after my dad died. Her sisters would fly into town and stay for a while, tell her she needed to take care of herself. Then they'd leave. People always left. It always came down to me and my mom.

So I took care of her. Until I couldn't.

After school I would do a load of laundry and vacuum the house. I learned how to cook a few things. Eggs and bacon, mostly—my aunties said I wasn't ready to be trusted with Grandma's secret macaroni 'n' cheese recipe yet. Mom just watched me like she was driving through a thick fog.

I loved her. But she was in pain and I couldn't reach her, and it hurt. My heart broke in inches before I lost her, too. She knew something had changed between us. She kept getting louder, trying to hold on to whatever we had.

She'd been loud a lot lately.

That day, all the blinds were closed again. Mom slouched on the couch, wearing the same dress she had on yesterday, fresh paint smeared across it. The whole house smelled like weed. Mom shivered. Her eyes were large. She was trying to numb whatever hurt so much in her. Or to quiet the voices in her head.

"Come here." She waved a cup toward me. "Have a drink with Momma."

I walked over to her, already knowing what she was sipping on before I sniffed her cup. An empty bottle of whiskey rolled away from her. When she kicked it out of my way. I took the cup. "I don't want to."

"Then give that back. Don't you waste my good medicine."

I froze. I didn't want to give it to her. I also

210

feared what she might do if I didn't. She snatched the cup from me so I didn't have to decide.

"You think you're better than me."

"I don't, Mom."

"You do. I can see it in your eyes." She took another drink. "You're not, you know. You're just like me."

I retreated to my room to change out of my school uniform into something comfortable to clean the house in.

She followed me from room to room as I cleaned, talking. Mostly to me. Sometimes to . . . them. Her voices. I'd long made my peace with them. They were every bit a part of my life as my aunties. Occasional visitors who dropped in, uninvited.

Eventually she settled in her "studio"—what she called the dining room when she was all amped up. I peeked around the corner. A plastic tarp covered the floor, laid down as an afterthought, only half covering anything, held down by buckets of paint. She glared at the wall like it had talked back to her.

"I see you up there, you know," she said without turning around to me.

"Where?" I asked, not sure if she was talking to me or one of them.

"At that fancy school."

Persons Crossings Public Academy was many things. Fancy was not one of them. "It's just school, Mom."

"Up there getting on honor roll. Miss Perfect Attendance."

"Those are good things, Mom."

"No, those are about showing me up. Showing me how perfect you are." She brushed a streak of red across the wall.

"I just want you to be proud of me, Mom." I stepped out from behind the doorframe, taking the chance of getting near her. She was painting over the mural she'd started the night before.

"Proud of what? What you going to do?"

"I don't know. Make the world a better place. Prettier. Like you do."

"That ain't how life works, baby girl. Things in this life just ain't fair. You can't win this game. They're all against you."

"They who?" Part of me hated letting her suck me into her rants.

"They." She waved her hands about. "Businesspeople. Politicians. Government. They're too big. You can't fight them. They won't let you make the world a prettier place."

She flung mustard-yellow paint against the wall. Frustrated, she smeared it about with her hands. Angry, frantic swirls.

Mom scared me.

I ran out of the house in my T-shirt and shorts. I didn't know what to do. Mom chased after me, screaming. I called 911 on my cell phone.

The neighbors came out to see what the yelling was about.

Red and blue lights flashed. The officers rushed toward us. I let one of the neighbors hold me as the officers talked to my mom. Soon an ambulance joined. Everything was so loud. The sirens. The neighbors. My mom. She screamed. First about them restraining her. Then she started accusing them of stealing her jewelry. As they were wheeling her into the ambulance, I caught her eye.

"Bella!" she yelled. "It will be all right, baby. Momma will make everything better. Come give your momma our special handshake."

213

I didn't move. The neighbor holding me patted my back.

Mom kept screaming my name until they slammed the doors of the ambulance shut.

"Schizophrenia. She's up in Marion. At the hospital." I study my hands. "She had a breakdown last year."

"I see." Lindsey scribbles on her papers. Summarizing my story in a few sentences. "Any grandparents?"

"No."

"Aunts, uncles, cousins?"

"None around here." I hate this. All my life spread out and dissected. Sounding all empty when it's described out loud.

"Any relative you can think of?" Lindsey keeps pressing.

I sniffle. My nose is runny. My eyes start to water, but I don't cry. Lowering his head to give me room, M wordlessly slides over a box of Kleenex. "When my mom went to the hospital, folks forgot about me. Didn't matter, though. I took care of myself."

"I can see that, but you shouldn't have had to." Lindsey closes her file. "Me and Mr. Paschall are going to chat for a bit. He's called in a Ms. Essence Campbell. Do you need anything?"

"You got any Oreos?" I try to sound cheery. Brave. Not embarrassed.

"I'll have some brought in."

True to her word, Lindsey walks in a few minutes later with a plate of Oreos. As the door opens and closes, I catch a glimpse of M in an animated conversation with people I can't see. I shift uneasily. My phone has reached 100 percent charge by the time they come back. They're like a jury returning with a guilty verdict, a parade of downcast, sour faces: M, Ms. Campbell, Lindsey, and her backup.

Getting out of my seat, I retreat to the back corner of the room near the toy chest. I cross my arms and fix a hard stare on my face. "Y'all got me figured out?"

"Bella, it's not like that." Lindsey waves her file in a sweeping gesture for me to join them at the table. I push off against the wall with a deep sigh, as if the effort of moving at all was an unfair ask and begin a slow walk back to them. "We're just trying to figure out the best next steps for you. We have thousands of kids in the system. We're overloaded and doing the best we can. No one wants to see you fall between the cracks again. Our usual first step would be to place you in emergency foster care. . . ."

"A holding cell." I back away a few steps.

Everyone takes a breath, preparing for me to make a run for it. Everyone except M. He holds his hand out. He doesn't look at me, only keeps it hovering there. I inch closer to the table. I don't sit back down, but I take his hand.

"It's not like that." Lindsey places the file folder on the table, noting how my eyes track its movement like it's a flamethrower aimed at my life. "Anyway, Ms. Campbell has been through the emergency foster care training. Do you know what a kinship relationship is?"

I shake my head.

"Kinship care is when someone steps in full-time to nurture and protect a child. Sometimes it's a relative, stepparent, or godparent."

"I don't got any of that," I whisper.

"Sometimes it's extended to a clan or tribe," Lindsey continues.

"Nope."

"Sometimes it's simply an adult who has a bond with a child. A friend."

An itch stirs in my belly. It's either the glimmer of hope or the grumble of hunger. This is the first time all night my stomach unclenches.

"Could that description fit your relationship with Ms. Campbell?"

"I . . . guess?" I don't know where to look.

"It's okay, honey. I ain't going nowhere." Ms. Campbell's voice is gentle and reassuring.

I shrug.

Lindsey walks around the table and sits on the edge closest to me. Reaching her hand up, she waits for my permission before she places it on my shoulder. "Let me get some paperwork for Ms. Campbell to sign and I'll schedule my visitation and we can get you out of here. Mr. Paschall, can you wait with your . . . client?"

M tips his leather hat to them as the rest leave. We sit in silence for a few minutes.

"Did you . . . know any of that, what I said about my family, already?" I ask.

"I kept my promise to you."

"Okay." Even though I believe him, I can't meet his eyes.

"I know all about Marion, though. It has a long history as an unforgiving place. . . ." M's voice trails off a bit. When I turn back to him, it's him that's avoiding my eyes. A sadness sits on him like a heavy coat, and he hums a tune I don't recognize, haunting and bitter. "My dad spent thirty years in the mental institution in Marion. And then at the VA Hospital before Reagan closed it down. He had schizophrenia, too."

"Really?" I collapse into the chair as if gravity finally catches up to me.

"I . . . don't like to talk about it. I think we have that in common."

All of a sudden I don't see the gruff old man ready to challenge anybody no matter how much money or power they have. I don't see the sharp mind or smart mouth. I see a little boy who's lost like me, who no one knows to look for.

"Do you ever wonder if they were broken?" I whisper. "My mom and your dad, I mean. Or if you might be?"

"I used to make up all sorts of reasons why he was gone. When I grew up, I decided that he had the gift of being a shaman. Like he had a different way of seeing the world that other folks couldn't always appreciate."

"I'm just so angry. All the time," I say.

"I know. Like you want to just punch things and yet you don't want it to eat you up."

"What did you do with it?"

"Learned to use it as my superpower." M smiles. "Focus my anger on things that need folks angry about them."

"But what does that look like for me?"

M leans close. "That's the real question to keep asking and you got to figure that out for yourself." M stands up and holds his arm out for me to take. "But if you don't mind the company of a dusty old man, I'll walk alongside you while you do."

"WELCOME HOME." Ms. Campbell steps aside once she's opened the door. "Well, I hope you come to see it as home one day."

I grunt half-heartedly in response.

There are so many adults in my life I know little about. They're like mysteries I've never had any interest in solving. And I'm not gonna lie: my usual interest in Ms. Campbell most times stopped at her candy bowl at her front door. So I've never had the chance to appreciate her home. But I also think that even if I had, it would still have been like walking into new territory now. I'm entering a new world, and I'm not sure of my place in it. I'm instinctively mapping escape routes. I heft my backpack higher on my shoulders. I haven't set it down yet.

Aaries follows behind, walking Thmei. She sniffs at Phineas, and the black cat hisses and raises a paw, prepared to swipe at her. As if she understands the threat, the dog gently eases her face toward the cat. She swats at the dog's nose a few times, another warning shot. But Thmei waits patiently, not moving, letting the cat get used to her being there. The cat doesn't quite warm up to her but allows Thmei to stand near her. Knowing that's the best she's going to get, Thmei slumps by the door, resting on her paws.

I should say something nice about the place. But I fight against every part of this moment like I'm on a forced march. I want to put in my earbuds to carve out some space to myself, still, Ms. Campbell wants my full attention.

Like with M's house, the front door opens into a living room with twin bookshelves standing along the wall like bored guards. One shelf slants down, its books slumped to the side. And unlike Mattea's show house by the park, every inch of Ms. Campbell's space feels lived in. A dividing half wall separates the room from the dining room, with pillars running the rest of the way to the ceiling to open up the space.

Shelves have been built into the dining room wall, turning it into a display cabinet. Inside the cabinet is a kind of memorial. For a child who lived only for a few months. Baby shoes, bonnet, birth certificate, dried graveside flowers. No ghosts were left behind for Ms. Campbell.

A section of wall remains uncovered by drywall, revealing bricks. It forms the backdrop for the television and gaming system. A leather sectional couch surrounds it. We pass Aaries's room, all funky socks and posters, and then Ms. Campbell's room, her door probably always half-open.

"The back bedroom is all yours. I had Aaries gather what was left of your things from the Ryder house and put them in there. You have your own bathroom." Ms. Campbell points toward the archway on the far side of the dining room.

I check the back door. "Even my own entrance."

"Well, I'd prefer you use the front door for security's sake. But yes. Doesn't mean you get to sneak in and out whenever you want, though." Her tone is light but also firm. Ms. Campbell's voice has a kind of hesitation to it. She doesn't want to scare me off with too much rule talk. "I don't have too many rules around here.

They mostly boil down to a ten o'clock curfew and check in with me to let me know where you're going. No boys or overnight guests. But I have no intention of playing warden. This is a home, not a jail."

As we head back to the porch, I don't say anything. Trust isn't easy to give or settle into, but I'm working on it.

"Looks like the whole squad is assembled." M flops down on an old wicker love seat. It wobbles as his weight settles into it.

"What squad?" I ask.

"Yours."

"I don't have a squad."

"You may want to look around this porch again. I don't see all that well, but I know a lot of people are in your corner ready to back your play."

I look at each of them. Ms. Campbell pats my shoulder. Aaries is playing on his phone, but I recognize that's mostly to keep from meeting anyone's eyes. M stares in my direction, his gaze not fixed on me in particular. Thmei edges along the porch acting like no one notices her. She gets close enough to nudge my elbow with her nose to get me to raise my arm so that she can nuzzle into me. There they are, the most random assembly of folks, and somehow they're on the verge of becoming my family. I can't take it. It's all too much. I dash back into the house and run to my new bedroom.

The system shuffled me from place to place after Mom went away. My aunties came in for a while and had me pack up all my stuff. They kept arguing over who would take me in, even in front of Child Services. Like I was a problem no one wanted.

The thing about being something no one wants to deal with is that I can depend on everyone believing that someone else is taking care of me. The few people left in my life think I must be with a relative they don't know about. Or that I must be lost in the foster care system. People don't ask too many hard questions if it's not their issue in the first place. And I was usually armed with vague answers. The key was to hint at something, enough to stop their probing but not so much to worry them to call Child Services.

The situation made me angry anyway.

I don't have the luxury to flit from dream to dream like my classmates. I can't worry about who likes me. I can't worry about what clothes to wear. I can't worry about the latest song or show or movie. I can only smile and pretend all the time. I can only work harder. I fight through my anxiousness. My worry. My hunger. I need to keep moving forward from one possible future to another. Like a wind shifting directions in a storm. Or colors blending together.

These days, when I get that lonely feeling, like I'm lost and nobody knows how to find me, I paint. And I've been painting a lot lately.

I balance on the corner edge of my bed. My bed. In my house. I can't wrap my mind around it. My two garbage bags of stuff stand next to a chest of drawers. Rummaging through what's left of my things, I sift through the remains of my old life. I find a framed picture of me and my mother. I forget when we took it, but it had been a good day. We were at a restaurant. I'm drinking my soda with a long straw while my mom makes a goofy face. Her giant Afro takes up a large portion of the picture. I keep coming back to her eyes, bronze with gold flecks. The inspiration for my mural of her.

Someone knocks at my door. I wipe away the tears from my cheeks and I crack it open.

"I'm heading over to M's," Aaries says.

"Okay," I say without any strength.

"Only feed her twice a day. Also, she'll beg like she's starving, but do not give her people food. She'll fart the rest of the day."

"What are you talking about?"

"Thmei. M wants her to stay over here. For you. A housewarming present."

"You mean M's dumping her on me." I open the door a little wider. "What makes you think I'm a dog person?"

"Everyone's a dog person."

"Ms. Campbell's clearly not."

"She just doesn't know it yet." Aaries flashed a grin. He's the kind of boy who thinks he's more charming than he is.

"She just going to let you drop a dog into her house?" I find myself leaning against the doorframe.

"That's Ms. Campbell's way if you let her."

"Takes in strays of all kinds?" I lower my eyes.

"Welcomes family of all kinds."

The next day, after letting me sleep in, Ms. Campbell grills hot dogs for lunch. She opens two different bags of potato chips but sets the bowl of salad in front of me. My first plan was to protest this entire arrangement by not eating. But Ms. Campbell doesn't pay one lick of attention to my silent protest. She keeps on eating and talking, passing food to me or reaching past me for more chips. Or fruit. Or Oreos, M's other housewarming gift. All the smells work their magic until finally I snack on the hot dog.

"She thinks she's slick," I whisper to Thmei as I grab a handful of chips. I vow to not like them. "We'll show her."

I share my meal with Thmei, slipping her bits of hot dog under the table. An hour later, her gas is so bad, Ms. Campbell makes me take her out for a walk.

Thmei's on a retractable leash that allows her to roam more freely. I don't think about where we're heading; I just let my feet, or sometimes Thmei's need to sniff or pee on something, guide my steps. Somehow, we still end up at Mr. Ryder's spot.

The house looks so different now, in that kind of way places do by day compared to at night. It no longer feels safe. Or like a home. The space has been violated. Still, I go around to the patio area and peel back the corner of plywood enough for Thmei to hop through.

Grover, Sarah, and Wes stare at me, accusatory. Or maybe I imagine that and their gazes are empty: no judgment, just wishing me well while their own fates remain in limbo.

Me and Thmei slink upstairs to find my room still a wreck. I sweep the area one more time to make sure Aaries didn't miss anything. Boys ain't exactly known for being thorough. Thmei rolls around in what's left of my bedroll. I find the shards of the sculpture I had made in my art class. The girl now missing her hands. The book broken in half. Picking up the pieces, I turn them over in my hands. I know I can fix it. I scoop the pieces into my backpack and tug the leash for Thmei to join me.

As we approach the stairs, Thmei growls. Slowing down, each step makes her more tense. I slacken the leash to allow her time to finish sniffing whatever caught her attention. My heart thuds hard. Forcing myself to take a deep breath, I go ahead and ease through the back door and then stop short.

Fury and Jared are waiting for me outside.

"FIGURED YOU'D COME back here sooner or later." Fury's half off his bike before I'm through the door.

"Just had to have patience." Jared takes two determined steps toward me. "I bet a sister could use a new journal. I wonder where I could get one of those."

Thmei bounds out of the house, stopping between me and them. The boys freeze.

"Right about now"—I hold up the retractable leash as if I might drop it—"you may want to rethink your life choices."

"Chill." Fury raises his hands. "Dag, chill for just a minute. We only here to talk."

"I don't believe you," I say.

"You'd think we'd let a dog stop us if the alternative

229

was facing an angry Pass?" Jared asks.

I believe Jared would sacrifice Fury in less than a heartbeat if the opportunity to gain something popped up. "Shoot your shot, then."

"Ms. Mattea wants to meet with you." Fury keeps his hands in plain sight and steps in front of Jared. Maybe to protect him in case I do decide to drop Thmei's leash. Maybe to take charge of this meeting so no misunderstandings occur.

"Since when you run errands for her?"

"Favor for a friend." Fury's words land like a gavel closing a case.

"What she want?"

"All she said was she wanted to make a peace offering."

I pretend to consider it for a moment, but I already know my curiosity is going to rule this decision. If they wanted to actually hurt me, they could do it now where there are few prying eyes. They must be under strict orders if Jared's managing to restrain himself. "I'll swing by her house."

"No," Fury says. "She said the library. One hour."

I'm not rash. I stop by M's on my way to see Mattea. Since I'm pressed and there's not an easy way to slide into the conversation, once I pop my head into his office I say almost absently, "Mattea summoned me to the library."

M stops clicking around on his keyboard. "You make it sound like a spell."

"Witches gonna witch. She sent Fury and Jared."

"She did?" M tries to not sound concerned but his eyes widen.

"You okay?" Aaries asks.

"I'm good. They . . ."

"What is it?" M asks.

"Before DCS scooped me up, someone had broke into my space at Mr. Ryder's house. Tossed my room. They took my journal with all my notes. Jared confirmed that it was him."

"They got your playbook?"

"Something like that. Just another way to try to stop me. That's why I'm off to meet with Mattea now."

"Alone?" Aaries has already taken several steps to the door.

"Yes, alone. I thought about bringing backup, but

M and Mattea can't help but get into it with each other and I need Mattea to make her play."

"Sounds fair," M says.

"It does?" Aaries asks. I appreciate his bodyguard routine and all, but they both need to give me room to do my thing my way, even if I get it wrong.

M nods. "We can be there in minutes if you need us."

∼

Just the idea of meeting with Mattea disturbs my mood so much, all I can see are the ghosts in the neighborhood. The jagged scars in the road. The sagging gutters. The drooping porches. Few people on the street, with the ones who are out eyeing each other with suspicion. Abandoned on lawns is discarded junk that no garbage man will ever take away. Even the refurbished Indianapolis Library No. 1 appears haunted around the edges.

The annex now seems gray and unwashed. Stopping at the receptionist's desk, the woman hard-eyes me without a word, the price of getting her chewed out over the TIF minutes mess. She grumbles something about Thmei, but since I ignore her and she didn't say anything directly to me, I wait in a chair far from her. I'm not going anywhere without backup. Especially not into Mattea's lair. Who knows what she has in there. Only a few minutes later, Mattea pops her head out of her office and waves me back.

"You came. And by yourself at that." She walks to her chair just fine without her cane.

"I got time."

When Thmei pads into view, Mattea frowns. I stop. Drawing the leash tighter, I bring Thmei closer to me. The dog cranes her neck back and forth as if following a ball we're tossing between us. Mattea relents. My dog's presence is not the hill worth her fighting over, which means there must be some other agenda item that's more important.

Mattea gestures to the empty chair on the other side of her desk.

"What did you want?" I pat my lap for Thmei to jump into, a decision I regret immediately. Thmei is too big for this. I still try to play things cool. Like her long nails aren't digging into my thighs while she gets comfortable. She scrambles into a position that leaves just her head propped over the desk.

"Right to business. I'm good with that." Moving

some papers out of licking range, Mattea then pours herself a cup of coffee before settling into her seat. She draws out the ritual to make me wait. Remind me of my place. "I wanted to settle this thing between us."

"This thing where you tried to sic DCS on me?"

"Be mad all you want, but the streets are no place for a little girl to be staying, no matter how grown she thinks she is." Mattea waves the air in front of her, wanting to reset her starting place. "This is what I mean. You've spent too much time around M. Picked up his annoying coyness. As well as his ability to disrupt just by showing up."

"All I wanted to do was something good for the neighborhood. An art program. Everyone else made it complicated."

"Me too. That's what I explained to the board after the CISC party. I told them that you had a good point. We're on the same side, you and I. We do need to showcase our local talent more. That's why I suggested you for our pilot project."

"What project?"

"A youth-organized art initiative. Like a community school. You find the talent, you work with the kids to organize yourselves. And you can have the overpass.

Paint over that 'Unfadeable' nonsense with art created by the community. Since it's only a pilot program, we can't give you much, say, ten thousand dollars."

This all comes at me sudden. Money. Power. Freedom. Options. That feeling of being overwhelmed starts to bubble in my stomach.

"Obviously, you'd have to have adult oversight."

"M?" I arch an eyebrow.

"Definitely not. Essence is fine, though, especially since she's on the governance board."

This is everything that I thought I wanted. I still want it. But something else nags at me. Mattea caving like this makes me so suspicious, the hairs on the back of my neck practically ache from trying to straighten. And I can't help thinking about my mom. How powerless she felt in her own neighborhood. Unable to fix anything. Not her marriage. Not herself. Not me. I want to accept the offer, if only to be able to do something my mom couldn't. Not to prove her wrong but to honor her. "This is . . . a lot. Can I have some time to think about it?"

"Absolutely." Mattea stands, clearly dismissing me. "You can get back to me tomorrow."

THERE ARE TIMES when I dream of leaving The Land. The west side. Indianapolis. Indiana. The Midwest. Maybe go to New York. Most of the kids at Persons Crossings Public Academy talk about going there or to LA to fulfill their dreams. Every now and then, someone might say Atlanta or, if they really wanted to stand out, Paris. Maybe Ghana. But I know most of us would never leave because we have family and friends right here.

Which is why I thought I was different. I had no family. No friends. No ties to this place. I could leave and go anywhere. Yet I find myself wandering over to M's house, knocking on his door, being let in by

Aaries—handing him Thmei's leash—and making my way back to see M.

"It smells like spring and armpits in here," I announce myself. A different jazz album is playing. It's a bit mellower. Not so on one. "Who's this?"

"Still Miles Davis. This time it's *Kind of Blue*." M has that look in his eyes. Like he's lost in big thoughts, trying to sort out how things connect.

"You must be in a good mood. You're less . . . you." I hover over his shoulder as he switches street views on his screens. The scene looks familiar, especially since I walk that stretch of Clifton Street almost every day. "What are you looking for?"

"Seeing how much the neighborhood has changed over the years." M's voice sounds tired. And sad. He rubs his eyes. "I'm using Google Maps street view like a time machine. Seeing the houses. The businesses. The neighbors. Our block is almost unrecognizable from how it used to be."

Studying the images on the monitors is like traveling through time. I'd forgotten about the beauty salon. Or the event space, which is now all boarded up. Or the old custom T-shirt place. Mom and I used to walk to the soul food place that was in the small business strip that became Clifton Corner.

"Why do you even bother?" I fall into the nearby couch. "Wake up every morning to fight against the government, the mayor, city council, businesspeople, and all the other folks with money and plans?"

"Our job isn't to fight them. If they all line up together, they'll win that fight every time. But we can hold them to account. Our job is to figure out how we are going to protect each other. Our property. Our community. Make sure the quality of life in our neighborhood improves."

I see what M means. I really want M's take on things but can't think of a good way to slide it into conversation. "So, my meeting with Mattea was interesting."

"Interesting. You all right?"

"Yeah. Maybe. She made me an offer. Ten thousand to start an art program." I can't even imagine what I'd do with all that money. It's like being offered the whole world.

"My, my, my. What did she say exactly?" M leans his chair back and bridges his long fingers.

"Just that. That she would give me ten thousand

dollars to start a youth-led arts program. The money would have to flow through Ms. Campbell, since she's an adult and is on the board. I can't help but think she's setting me up."

"Sounds about right. Straight out of her usual playbook. It also has the side benefit of dragging Essence into a potential mess at the same time," M says.

"What do you mean?" The idea of getting Ms. Campbell into trouble doesn't sit well with me. This is like playing chess in the dark. I can't see much of the board, and I know my queen is in danger.

"It's like you said. Mattea knows something. Or the people she reports to have information about what's coming down the road that she got a heads-up about."

I snap my fingers. "Their upcoming board meeting."

"Hmm." M strokes the wisps of his beard. "Not bad. The board of directors has to show up for it. The occasional city-county council member, too. It's their official oversight meeting. While you out here making waves by connecting too many dots."

I think about my missing journal. "So they're . . . coming for me?"

"Carrot before the stick. A sure sign that you're being effective is that someone in power comes along to offer you a job. A good job. Well-paying."

"Is that bad?"

"No. Not at all. It's money put into good hands to do good work."

"But?"

"But the other side is that you'd be too busy to do the effective thing you were doing before."

I scoot to the edge of the couch. "Is that why you quit being a lawyer?"

The question catches M off guard. The way he shifts, he might as well announce his intention of dodging the question. "What are you going to do?"

I let him keep his reasons to himself. For now. "I don't know. It's tough dealing with people who look like how a grandma should but who do nothing but make excuses and lie all the time. And I mean all. The. Time. But ten stacks is a lot of money."

"For anyone, much less someone with no bills." M chuckles. His eyes grow even more cloudy-looking than usual, like he's floating off on a dream. "Back when I was in college, right after I had just broken up with my girlfriend, I was storming about the campus in a real mood. Now, I was one of only a few Black faces in that whole place. One night I was walking to the library when the English department dean bumps into me. He asks me for my ID, like I was out of place and had no reason to be there. Keep in mind, I had been there, in his school—practically in his department—for nearly three years.

"'A lot of other students passed you, but you didn't ask anyone else for their ID,' I tell him.

"'Let me see your ID,' he says. 'Unless you want me to get the police to talk with you?'

"Like that was supposed to be some kind of threat. So, I stand there and just stare at him dead in the eye. A campus security officer finally walks by and the dean calls him over. He explains the scenario to him, so the security guard asks for my school ID and I show it to him. Just him, not the dean.

"'Yeah, he goes here,' the guard says.

"'You could have just said so,' the dean says to me. 'Saved us all some time.'

"'Nah, you wanted to waste my time, so I decided to waste yours. And I'm rich with time,' I say.

"The dean stomped off. He was on the other side of mad.

"'That's the dean,' the officer says to me. 'You shouldn't talk to him like that.'

"'He can't just go around harassing folks. Forget him.'

"I was still feeling some sort of way later that night, so I take my rage and write a long letter to the editor of the school newspaper. Lots of folks read it, pass it around. I hit the administration's radar in a big way. And after that, people were like, 'Don't mess with M.' You need to do something to make them stand up and take notice of you. On your terms."

I think back to what M said about being judged and how to navigate it. He's so casual about, I don't know, Black things. My mom was rarely so direct, especially when Dad was around. Like she was protecting me from it. Being around M, I find everything just feels calmer. Like I have space to mess up.

"Two things. One, I think we're past a letter-writing situation." I hold up my fingers to count them off. "And two, I bet you didn't just say, 'Forget him.'" I grin.

"See? There's another important lesson for you. Always consider your audience."

I lie down on the couch. As if the act pinged her

radar, Thmei runs into the room and jumps onto it, forcing me to slide over. My foot taps along to the music. There are so many angles to this puzzle, most I either don't understand or don't even know about. I need to poke them in the eye, do something unexpected to get them off-balance and playing on my terms.

"Hey, M, if I have this video of the James Sidney Hinton Park, how can I make sure the right people see it?"

"What are you trying to do?" M asks. "You have your arts program if you want."

"This is bigger. She needs to be taken down."

"Then a good first step might be making sure the right people see it. But you'll be dealing with folks with power. That scare you at all?"

"No." I blink a couple times. "Maybe."

"What are you going to do when power pushes back?"

"You mean when they send the stick?" I squish into the back of the couch while I think. "Yeah . . . I don't know if I can do this."

"When you work with what you have, you always can."

I let the words settle on me, but they don't do much. "I don't know. I need to learn more. Maybe if I can dig up dirt on the folks involved."

A mischievous grin reveals M's yellowed teeth. "Well, if you'll allow me to help you there, I can show you how to do some homework."

START **WHERE YOU** are with what you have.

The greatest power a neighborhood has is the people who live there. Just thinking about all the gifts and talents on the block makes me so proud. These are my neighbors. I want them to learn about each other and see what's going on. Support the work that's already being done.

"Do you know what a TIF is?" I ask.

"It's some tax thing," Ben Taylor says.

"Who you fooling? As soon as folks start talking tax credits, your eyes start glazing over," Georgia says.

"People just go around making things unnecessarily complicated," Ben adds.

"That's what I keep saying!" I say.

"It's all the same game: takes money to make money," Georgia says.

"Taking money is the point," I say. "We have a lot of money right here in the neighborhood. Someone's eating while making sure we don't know."

"What do you mean?" Georgia huddles closer to me.

I run down the money game as best I can. I keep waiting for them to give me a *that's so cute, look at her talking grown stuff* look. But they don't. They listen. Especially by the time I get to the one and a half million dollars part and the school no one asked for. They're really interested. And getting a little mad. Georgia keeps glancing at the light posts or the sidewalks, all the things that have needed fixing for years. That's the reaction I want.

We've been forgotten. It's like the city and businesses decided we weren't here, or we weren't good enough, and left. We're broken. And then after years of neglect they decide we're ripe for them to fix us. Like they're the heroes and not the problem. We've been fixing with what we have the entire time.

After Georgia feeds me cookies and lemonade, I

continue down the block. My goal is to talk to whoever I see. Knock on a few doors of folks I know. In
preparation for it, M had me researching the entire
morning. I had to create a PowerPoint on who the
mayor was, the city-county council, school board, all
the way down to the TIF governance committee. He
was determined for me to know who the true players
are. It was like the worst kind of homework. I mean,
I get I should know who the mayor is. That's basic.
But he had me pull up the city-county council members. A lineup of smiling suits with hungry eyes.

While I was looking folks up, I ran across an old
picture of Mattea standing with a woman named
Davina Odom. I Googled Mattea and the name
Odom. Mattea's mother. As I walk, I think about the
license plate that read, "Ms. Odom." Interesting.

With my sketchbook tucked under my arm, I
check down the block before walking out in the open.
My ears wide open, listening for bikes or Jared's wild
whooping and hollering. A nice breeze trails me, but
my heart still races. I can't help the feeling of being
followed.

I chat with the bus stop ladies, collecting more
names and contact information. I keep spreading the

word about the annual meeting. There's an energy building. Like in a basketball game when one team suddenly gets hot. Plays better. Perfectly in sync. A kind of magic.

A twig snaps behind the bushes next to me. My hand reaches for my Mace.

"Relax, it's just me." Aaries creeps out with his hands up. "Easy with your trigger finger."

"What are you doing here?"

"Following you."

"Why? Don't think I can do this on my own?"

"You stay steady hostile." Aaries lowers into a crouch. He studies the street. A car drives down Clifton, a little too slow for my taste. "Can we talk over here? Less visible."

I almost make a crack about me not going behind some bush with a boy, but something about his voice seems urgent. The car's brake lights flare.

"What's wrong?" I peel around the corner, behind the row of hedges. "Why did M send you?"

"He didn't. Not exactly. He believes to do this work, you have to make mistakes. That's how we learn. But this is about safety."

"I can take care of myself."

"No doubt. But it's okay to have backup. Especially when—" Aaries stops talking. He tracks the car as it idles along the street.

"There's something you're not telling me."

"There's a bounty on you."

"What sort of bounty?"

"Jared and Fury hunting you. The Paschall crew wants to make your life . . . difficult."

"A bully's gonna bully." I guess they can organize, too. I can't help but imagine a social network for them.

"But out here, you know how quick things can jump off."

"So you playing the hero?"

"I'm strictly security. Like an umbrella, to keep you dry so you can do what you do."

"What'd I tell you from the jump?"

"Sidekick." He smirks, a smile so easy I almost relax.

I'm skeptical, but Aaries holds his hands up again, signaling that he'd back off if asked.

"All right, we can try this. But I'm in charge."

"Was that ever in doubt?" Aaries makes sure the street's clear before waving me out from the bushes. "What's your next move?"

"You think I been out here collecting email addresses and spreading the word about the annual meeting for my health?" I pat my sketch pad. "We're heading to the library. I have a message to send."

THE ANNUAL MEETING is jumping. By early afternoon, many of the neighbors received the email of footage. Everyone along the chain from the UNWA governance board up to key people in the mayor's administration received an anonymous email containing video footage of the James Sidney Hinton Park project.

I may have also made a TikTok asking questions about where the money went. About safety concerns. I spliced in a scene of Mattea and them dancing at the CISC reception.

We stroll up to Indianapolis Public Library No. 1. I walk between M and Ms. Campbell, with Aaries behind me playing Secret Service or whatever. I hope

Thmei's not chewing up all the stuff in my room

"Look at all these people," Ms. Campbell says.

"More than you expected?" I ask.

"More than . . . ever. It's usually not bigger than a regular meeting. Usually less because it's mostly a numbers report."

"With no snacks," I add.

"We're over budget. Again," she says.

"I'm not surprised."

"Members of the city-county council are here," M says.

"Yeah. I got word that several members of the city-county council have 'expressed concerns' about how the governance board has been operating," Ms. Campbell says.

"That means a lot of eyes. Especially those that control the money." M glances around as if noting the people around him. Aaries keeps whispering names to him.

"I think a couple reporters are here," Ms. Campbell says. "Are you nervous?"

"A little," I say. "But M's had me practicing the last couple days."

Ms. Campbell bends to meet my eyes. "You got this."

She starts to turn away when I realize that I've tugged at her arm. I didn't mean to. It's more of an instinct. I hold out my thumb up. Confused, she just stares at me for a second, but she must read something in my eyes. She mirrors the gesture. I press my thumb to my chest and hold it there until she does the same thing.

"My heart," I say.

"My heart," she echoes. The corners of her eyes glisten. "I . . . need to find my seat."

She wraps her vitiligo-tinged hands around mine and gives them a squeeze.

When M and I arrive at the door, the truck mechanic sits there instead of the usual bouncer. Up close, he's easily M's elder. The old man points to his scalp.

"M, I think he wants you to take off your hat," I say, unable to hide my grin.

"You've got to be kidding me," M says.

"Respect the house," the old man says, as if the building's a church.

"Yes, sir." M removes his fedora and runs his hand through what's left of his Afro.

I stifle a snicker.

"We all have to respect our elders," M says.

"That's funny, considering what we're about to do," I whisper as we head in.

"We can respect their wisdom and experience and still challenge their ideas. That's the only way to make room for new ideas to break through."

By the time the meeting rolls around, people crowd the library space to standing room only. The air conditioner barely works on its best day; now it's packed up and gone on vacation. Folks fan themselves with anything handy. M slips into a seat, if you can call his wobbling, side-to-side entrance sneaking, sitting three-fourths of the way back. He grabs an aisle seat so that he can have a great view of the show. Aaries sits closer to me, like a mother hawk guarding her nest, toward the end of M's row. The good reverend is up in the front row.

Mattea, Walls, and Ms. Campbell walk in like judges about to hear arguments in a case. Perfect for what I have in mind. Mattea does a slow roll to her seat, making an extra show with her cane. Taking her seat, she quickly makes judicious use of her gavel, pounding away, since getting so many people to shut up is worse than the cafeteria at school. With folks still finding their seats, things are chaotic enough for no one to notice me. I make my way to the microphone stand.

"Hi, my name is Bella Fades. I had a few questions about—"

"Young lady." Mattea raises her gavel. "We appreciate your enthusiasm. In fact, it always pleases us when young people get involved in the process, but we have a lot to get through tonight. We'll try to leave time for questions at the end of the meeting."

I remain at the microphone, unmoving. "I just wanted to save the committee some time by telling them who sent that email that brought everyone here today, but I guess I'll go wait in back."

"Wait." Mattea's eyes widen with mild panic, like she's been caught with her hand still on the mayor's wallet. "How do you know who sent the email?"

Turning around, I look for M, who shrugs innocently. Returning my attention to Mattea, I clear my throat. "Because it was me."

"You . . . ?"

255

"And as I was saying, I had a few questions to ask because I'm confused—a lot of us are confused—as to how things work around here." The mic whines when I step so hard to it.

"I, for one, would love to hear the young lady's questions," Ms. Campbell says. The tone of her voice dares Mattea to try to shut me down in front of all the folks I brought. "If they are as well thought-out as those in the email, it might actually speed things along. That is, if the point of this meeting is transparency in front of the community."

Mattea stares Ms. Campbell down. She must know I'm staying with her by now. News travels fast on these streets. But it keeps her off-balance. I can use that. Finally she says, "We can allow a few minutes for opening questions to catch everyone up."

I consult my notes. M and Aaries spent hours yesterday grilling me for practice. But I'm still nervous. I feel like a lawyer at her first trial. I stay focused. I'm coming for her.

"If I understand it, a TIF is sort of like a community bank account."

"It's a bit more complicated than that." Mattea takes a drink from her bottled water. She has a smug look, like she's amused by the antics of the little girl at the mic.

"Yeah, grown-ups usually make things as complicated as possible." I look up from my notes. "How does money come out of this community bank account?"

"No one gets money without coming through the board." Mattea shifts in her seat, aware that her answers are very much on the record.

"That's how it's supposed to work."

"Yes."

"How does money get in the account in the first place?" I ask. "I'm only in middle school and I just want to understand."

"The city holds a percentage of the property taxes and—"

"Hang on, I'm only in middle school. I'm trying to figure out why I should care here. Taxes: they sort of like collecting an allowance. That I get. The city gets an allowance that we pay." I shrug like it almost makes sense.

"Yes, and it puts your allowance into a sort of bank account for the neighborhood to use to improve itself."

"So that we can handle our own problems, since

we live here, know what's wrong, and can choose the projects most important to us."

"Exactly."

"How much does the city put into this account each year?" I raise my notes, my pen ready to either add to them or check figures.

"About . . ." Mattea scrambles to her folder of papers. Caught off guard, she flips through the pages of her own notes. "Seven hundred thousand dollars."

A wave of murmurs sweeps across my neighbors.

"Who asked for the school you all are proposing?" I change topics. I don't want her to see my questions coming. The best way to trip people up is to come at them one way so they think they know where you're going, then change the line of questioning to catch them slipping. It's the standard interrogation technique Mrs. Fitzgerald uses. Mattea obviously hasn't been drilled by a middle school principal recently. "Wait, not 'all.' According to the minutes, it's always Ms. Larrimore and Mr. Walls outvoting Ms. Campbell."

"It's no secret that the public school system is failing—"

"Oh, believe me, I know. I'm in it." I'm not gonna

lie. I really wish I wore glasses. It'd be good for my look if I could peer over them at her like I don't believe anything she's trying to sell me. "Now, if I understand things right, schools are supported by property taxes, too, right?"

"Yes."

"That's got to be great for us, since Golden Hill is right in our backyard." I keep my back to her while she answers.

"They're not counted for this neighborhood."

"Oh, that's too bad." I pretend to be shocked by this news. The crowd smiles with me, encouraging me. "So, you never answered me, who asked for the school?"

"Hold on, hold on. This isn't an episode of *Law & Order*." Mattea bangs her gavel. "How are you going to come in here and question grown folks like they in court?"

"Because this is a community meeting. A public conversation where anyone from the community can ask questions. I live in this community." I look up to lock eyes with her. "Do you?"

"Of course I do. You of all people should know." Mattea glares at me.

"We'll come back to that."

My smirk rattles Mattea for a second, but she covers it up just as quickly. She raises her gavel to cut me off.

"Let the girl talk," a voice yells from the back of the room.

I smile, recognizing M.

"If it will speed things along, I'll cede all of my time to Miss Fades," Ms. Campbell says. I hadn't told her what M and I were up to so that she wouldn't be put in a spot where she'd have to lie or try to cover for me. I didn't want to risk getting her in trouble, even though I can almost hear her say, "Protecting you is what I'm supposed to do," just like my mom used to say.

Thinking about how much she cares for me makes me bold enough to turn to face Clarence Walls next to her. "Did *you* ask for the school?"

"No, I . . ." He glances back and forth. I know that look. When you wish you had a baby brother or sister to blame for what you just did.

"Did you ask for the James Sidney Hinton Park?"

"Like I was trying to say, no, I—"

I snap my fingers. "That's right, my mistake.

You asked for a building project. Built you that nice, shiny Clifton Corner. The funds for that center, did they come from our bank account?"

"Um, yes." He takes out his pocket square and wipes the sweat off his forehead.

I all but lick my lips at that. "Look, as I understand it, a good developer never uses they own money to do construction. We ain't hatin' on your hustle. That's just good business."

"Thank . . . you," Walls says like a man trying to walk through Ms. Campbell's backyard but not sure where to step because Thmei's been doing her business back there.

"Then you were asking for a parking lot to go with your Clifton Corner. Because you didn't expect the success your center would have."

"Yes."

"Which is kinda sus considering how little traffic comes through. But you even got the church going into partnership with you."

"Yes." Walls risks a glimpse toward the good reverend, who goes against his natural instincts and shrinks away from the spotlight tracking his direction.

"You are good at finding partners. Cooperation gets things done, right?"

"Yes, I'd say so." Since it seems like I'm easing up on him, Walls settles back and straightens his jacket with pride.

"Where is the parking lot going to go?"

"We don't know yet. We're still exploring options."

"Have you met Mr. Taylor?" I step to the side so that he can get a clear view of the Taylors, front and center in the audience. To make sure everyone knows them, I wave. Georgia waves back. Ben nods.

"Yes." Walls runs a finger inside his tight collar.

"I bet you have. He been in the neighborhood for decades. He and his wife are fixtures in the community. Did you know they been married for forty-three years?"

"No, I didn't."

"Their whole marriage spent right here in The Land." I pause for effect, making sure I have the full attention of the city-county council members. "That's what folks around here still call this place you renamed Northwest Planners."

Mattea smacks her gavel. "That's about enough, young lady."

262

"I just don't want anyone to be confused. It gets easy to do that when you keep renaming things. Like you. Mattea Larrimore. Have you always gone by Larrimore?"

"Yes." That catches her off guard, hopefully distracting her enough to forget her charge at me.

"We'll come back to that."

"No, I don't think we will." Mattea rises from her seat. "We've had about enough out of you."

"Let the girl talk!" M yells again. A few other voices echo him, a swelling murmur that rises like an Amen in church.

Mattea's eyes dart all over the place, the way a new substitute teacher starts to panic when too many folks act up at once. She sits back down, probably to give herself time to figure out her best play, but I take the moment to go all in.

"Mr. and Mrs. Taylor own that corner lot, the one with the Village Bodega on it. They have to close it. We lose our last market, making a bigger food desert in The Land. But you knew that, didn't you, Mr. Walls? Do you know who got it shut down?"

"I . . ." Like he's just drifted into the deep side of the pool and is slowly going under, he looks over to the city-county council to throw him a life preserver. No one even looks his way.

"Yup. *You.*" I step away from the mic so that everyone can see him. Truly see him. "But that's not what I really want to ask. See, we know you a well-connected guy. Seem to know everyone. Do you know Kevin Paschall?"

The entire room grows ice still as everyone waits to see how he will answer the question.

Ms. Campbell and Mattea all but shrink away from him like he's contagious.

"We all do."

"What does he do for a living?"

His eyes pop so wide open, I think they might fall out his head. Poor Clarence squirms in his chair. "He's in . . . real estate."

"Okay, we'll go with that." I wink to everyone. "Would you say you're friends?"

"We know each other."

"Pretty well, I'd say. You took in a couple of his people for your neighborhood mentoring program. The same people that may have had . . . an intense conversation with Mr. and Mrs. Taylor about selling their property." As I turn my attention to the city-county people, I catch a glimpse of Fury and Jared posted up against the wall. "Allegedly. Ain't no snitches up in here and can't no one identify those two fools. Whoever they might be. But hypothetically, could such a conversation have happened because you asked a friend for help?"

Clarence hovers over his microphone to clearly enunciate the word. "No."

"That's the right answer. For them." I sweep my arm toward the city officials. "But we all know how the game works at our level."

The room erupts. Mostly folks in agreement, but the city-county council members stir, uncomfortable. Grumbling as they distance themselves as much as possible from the mess rather than risk getting splashed with it.

"Okay, that's it, young lady." Mattea hammers her gavel like she's auditioning to be a drummer. "I'm not going to have you come in here and turn these proceedings into a circus."

"What gives you the right to say that?"

"I'm the head of this board," Mattea growls into the microphone. "Make no mistake, young lady. I have the final say."

"I don't think you do." I casually take a bottled water from my backpack. I suck it while basking in the heat of her glare.

"Why is that?" Mattea asks.

"You don't live here." I set my bottle down in my empty chair next to the aisle and collect my notes. "You certainly don't stay in that house. According to public records, Mattea Larrimore lives in Westfield. Wait." I make a show of checking my notes. "Mattea Odom, Ms. Odom being your maiden name, lives up in Westfield. Davina Larrimore, your daughter, is the registered owner of the house by the park. You don't even live here anymore. Like every other vulture, you just swoop in when there's something in it for you. So I don't think you have the standing to object to anything."

Mattea raises her gavel, but before she can, I glare at her.

"Bang that gavel one more time."

"Let the girl talk!" M yells.

"Let the girl talk," Aaries echoes from his side of the room.

"Let the girl talk." Georgia Taylor joins them.

I take a moment to feel their encouragement.

Chancing a look around, I search for M's face. He nods. Taking a deep breath, I gather myself and prepare for one last run.

"I just have a few last questions. Is our community account current with the city?"

Mattea adjusts her blouse collar. She and Clarence must go to the same tailor because both of their shirts seem too tight. "We're two years in arrears."

"That's fancy talk for you owe the city money, right?" I ask. "Like somehow more money's been used up than has been paid in."

"Something like that."

"Y'all just don't stop spending. Heck, I wouldn't either if I'm spending other folks' money. Ten Gs here, ten Gs there: that kind of accounting could get someone in trouble if they're not careful. I mean, someone could accept ten grand—you know, like that pay off you tried to offer me—and, if they're *not* Mr. Walls, end up on the hook for it or something."

Mattea's eyes focus on me like cold lasers, but I raise my hands like I'm backing off.

"One last question. What does . . . ?" I check my notes again. Pointing to a word on my paper, I meet her eyes again. "'Sunsetted' mean?"

She goes several shades paler. "Where did you see that?"

"In the minutes from the governance committee meeting. The public minutes? Someone mentioned that the TIF will be sunsetted in two years."

"It means"—Mattea angles her body away from the city council members—"the city will close it out."

"So, no more bank account," I emphasize.

"No more bank account."

I take another swig from my bottle of water to allow the words time to sink in. "So, by the time any money is due back—from an overdrawn account, at that—there won't be an account to pay it back to. Making it free money for *some* folks. I need to find me a bank like that."

The crowd's ready to boil over. Some of them are out of their seats, demanding explanation.

"You're misconstruing the facts." Mattea fumbles about like she can't remember how her gavel works. "That's not how it—"

"I'm sure it's not, 'cause when *we* out here fall into 'arrears,' bill collectors start blowin' up our phones!" I shout. The crowd howls with laughter at that shot. "If anyone remembers to collect, who gets the money?"

"The city."

"Not The Land." Okay, maybe I *have* watched one too many law shows, but I'm really feeling this moment. "I think y'all forgot who you work for. Well, I haven't. We're here. We live here. We love here. The people of The Land." Dropping my sketch pad onto the chair next to me, I begin to pull out pages and pass them around. My sketches of the people in the neighborhood. My portraits reimagining them, what they could be. The Taylors. The old mechanic. The teacher in Bertha Ross Park. The girls at the bus stop. The bike guys. M as a wizard. Even Jared and Fury.

I approach Walls but don't block the spotlight he loves so much.

"So, just to recap: Mr. Walls received loans from the neighborhood, our bank account, which he used to begin his development empire. By the time the original loan is due back, that money flows to the city, where it can be given out anywhere, no longer marked for The Land."

I take a couple steps over so that I can stare Mattea in the eyes.

"Ms. Odom here"—I emphasize her real last name—"got cash out of the same account to build a park when we already have a park that doesn't get enough. We're still not sure who asked for the new park, but someone got the better part of a hundred thousand dollars out of it. Someone—again, we not sure who—has come back to ask for more money to finish the janky job. Another—or maybe the same—someone has asked for even *more* money from us to build a school when we already have a school—my school—that already doesn't get enough."

I turn around to face my neighbors.

"I guess all I want to know is who is doing all this asking and where's all this money going? Was it any of y'all?"

"Naw," they cry out. M follows with a "heck naw" once the murmurs start to settle.

"I'd ask if it was any of y'all," I say to the city officials. "But don't worry, you all are guests at this meeting and I won't put any of you on the spot. But this whole process stinks. Can someone please act like you have our best interests in mind? That's what

270

I want. That's all any of us want." I back away from the microphone stand. Then I remember and step back to it. "My name is Bella Fades. But you can call me Unfadeable."

The crowd bursts into a round of applause. Mattea strikes her gavel, attempting to gather order. Several of the city-county council members slink out the nearest exits as the crowd surges to confront Walls and Mattea with a wave of questions. Clarence retreats quickly, before anyone thinks to stop him. I guess he's been taking some exit specialist lessons from yours truly. But folks know what he's about now. Mattea stands her ground to argue and explain.

I guess the meeting is adjourned.

"How'd I do?" I ask Ms. Campbell as she slips around the swarming crowd. They have no interest in her. They know who was and wasn't fighting for them.

"You did great, baby. Made a big mess of things. I may be home late cleaning up some of this." Ms. Campbell takes out her phone. "I hope you don't mind, but I took some shots of you in action up there. Making me so proud."

I don't know where to put my eyes. Her bright,

beaming face is too much to take in. But I kinda love it, too. "Is it all right if M takes me out to Burger King?"

"Of course. You've earned it." Ms. Campbell lingers for a heartbeat. "When I get home, I was thinking that maybe I could add your cell to my family plan. You know, just so you ain't got to keep worrying about your minutes. Only if you want."

"I'd . . . like that."

She nods and I watch her go back toward the crowd.

"What makes you think I want to take you to Burger King after the show you just put on?" M asks as he steps up behind me.

"Because now"—I don't bother to face him—"I know you actually want to buy me two Oreo pies to go with it."

"And I'm done arguing." He shrugs and holds his elbow out.

EPILOGUE

WE DID IT.

I help organize a group of neighbors to redo the tire wall in the park. While the Taylors plant flowers donated from their garden, the bus stop girls remove each tire, repaint it, and restack them, turning the entire mound into an art piece. The old mechanic heads up the group rebuilding and restoring the slide and swing set. A couple of dads in particular have already been too extra with the equipment and now the entire thing looks like a fort that can withstand a month-long attack.

The scene reminds me of M's first lesson: start where you are with what you have. I wanted an art project to bring the community together. I thought I had to get funding from somewhere, but it turns out we had everything we required already: each other. Neighbors chipping in, working together, picking up the pieces to make something new out of them, rather than just abandoning the tire wall. The park. The neighborhood.

I'm busy with a new art piece. Ms. Campbell bought me this set of marker paints and I'm trying them out by illustrating a sign for the new bike shop: *Bikerz*. Thmei stalks the park about as far as her strained leash allows, sniffing at everything or rolling in the grass. Her toenails pop in the sunlight. I painted them with glitter polish. I stand back to admire my work on the sign. Checking the time—it's ten till noon—I hand over the sign to Fyzle, grab my backpack, and begin the hike back to M's house.

It's one of the rare Indiana summer days free of the kind of mugginess that feels like police swarming the block. It's not too hot out, and the light breeze makes the day downright pleasant. I wave at Ms. Campbell as I walk by. Her "everyone contributes to the community of the house" speech replays itself in my head as a reminder that I still have dishes to do when I get home.

Home. I'm still letting the word truly sink in.

Aaries greets me at M's door with a stupid grin on his face, like he wants to sell me a mixtape.

I play-elbow him in the side. "What?"

"Nothing."

"What?" I ask, still suspicious that he's up to something.

"He's waiting for you."

I unleash Thmei, who scrambles like she's never been on these wood floors before, slamming right into the wall because she's so excited to keep up with me.

"You heard the latest?" M asks without spinning around.

"No, what?" I slide onto the couch. Thmei hops into my lap once she's done sniffing at a pizza box, confirming that it—and the other two boxes—are empty.

"'A local businessperson has stepped down from his neighborhood's governance committee due to scandal,'" M reads from one of his monitors. "I love this part. 'A city auditor has locked down all the accounts due to the questions raised. The investigation into any wrongdoing may take several months.' But it helps if you have connected friends."

"What do you mean?"

"Even though the charter school was derailed, Mattea Larrimore announced that she's been selected to chair the board for the school once they find a new location for it.'"

"So the school's going to happen anyway, just not as fast as they wanted." My voice deflates. We did a whole lot of work only for them to win anyway.

"Or where they wanted. Plus, it won't be funded in the shadows through back-end deals."

"Yeah, but Mattea climbs the ladder." I sag into the couch.

"I don't know if I'd call moving from the governance board to the school board any kind of climb." M spins his seat around. "What's on your mind?"

"Why do you . . . we, anyone . . . bother? I know what you said about community holding people to account, but after all this, nothing much has changed. What's the point?"

"That's a great question. A hard one." M runs his fingers through his beard. "For starters, you threw a monkey wrench into their plans. You dug into their business, shined a light into their darkness, and reminded people in The Land—who felt powerless and without much hope—that they had a powerful voice."

"I guess." I hug a cushion to my chest. A frustrated Thmei attempts to nuzzle her way under my arm anyway.

"You guess? Did you miss the part about them having to find a new location? Meaning them not tearing down the old Write On spot. Or the Ryder house. Now, make no mistake, some folks ain't too happy with you for those very same reasons."

"You're smiling. Is that a good thing?"

"I can't help myself. When you do good work, the fight never ends. But you should also celebrate the wins you get."

"Mm." I make a noncommittal grunt, not quite convinced.

M scoots back from his desk and reaches for a shelf, his hand fumbling until he finds what he's looking for. "I got you something."

He hands me a box. I open it. It's a stack of business cards in a fancy case. The cards read:

BELLA FADES
Neighborhood Investigator

"This for real?" I turn a card over in my hand. "I . . . have something for you, too." Opening my backpack, I pull out a small canvas. "I know you can't see too well, but it's a portrait. You, me, Ms. Campbell, Aaries, and Thmei at a concert at Mr. Ryder's house. Grover Washington, Sarah Vaughan, and Wes Montgomery all performing. I imagine it's one of Miles's songs. I hope you like it."

"It's perfect." M holds the painting. "We're officially like Batman and really insecure Robin."

"That's all right, M. One day you might make a good Batman." I close the lid and slip the cards into my pocket. "Can I call Aaries 'Alfred'?"

"That's between you and him." M swivels his chair back around, setting my painting next to his monitors. He says in a low mumble, "You all right. I guess."

I sneak up to his chair and wrap my arms around his neck. "You all right, too."

ACKNOWLEDGMENTS

This book wouldn't be possible without the mentorship and example of Imhotep Adisa, Leah (whose bravery and perseverance always inspire me), and the rest of the Kheprw Institute, as well as Wildstyle and the rest of the folks in the community who care and do good work. Who organize and resist. The candy ladies. The Big Mommas. The gardeners. The artists. The car repair guys. The activists. The political rock throwers. And all the folks who contribute to the abundance of the quality of life in the neighborhood.

Phoebe Harp, my early reader whose advice to "make this less boring" will make her a great future editor. And the rest of my students, who are too many to list but who it's been my honor to know and love.

William Ryder. Mari Evans. All of our neighborhood artists in whose shadow I work.

Outreach, who never stops being a champion for homeless teens.

My agent, Jen Udden; my editors, Claudia Gabel and Stephanie Guerdan, who never stopped pushing me and what this story could be.

My wife, Sally. And my favorite usual suspects, Reese and Malcolm.